Handcuffed

NICOLETTE JOHNSON

Day-N-Night Publishing

Day-N-Night Publishing

ISBN: 978-0-578-24577-5

Library of Congress Control Number: 2021902985

Cover Photo © 2021 www.gettyimages.com. All rights reserved - used with permission.

PRINTED IN THE UNITED STATES OF AMERICA

Dedication

*To my friends and family whose encourage-
ment gave my inner soul a voice.*

Thank you

Chapter 1

Lily

I love the smell of the marsh, salty yet sweet mist splashing my senses with springtime. I love watching the sunrise after working twelve-plus-hour shifts of pure hell. The streets have been so busy with missing young girls popping up everywhere in downtown Savannah. What's scary is they all look like my beautiful baby sister. Long brown hair and hazel eyes make up her striking physique. We both got our eyes from our dad and long, wavy hair from our mom. I miss my mom and dad, but I have to stay strong for my sister, Amelia. She needs me. I am my sister's keeper.

The girls are so young. So far there are two missing girls according to the news, but I know better. There are four girls, but the news refuses to mention two of the girls because they are prostitutes, street walkers.

"Lily," Amelia calls out, breaking my daydreaming. "Lily!"

"Yes, Amelia?" I say, knowing that if I don't answer she will continue to yell my name.

"Can I borrow one of your cars today? My car is still in the shop for an oil change and brake shoe replacement. I have clinicals all day today," Amelia says.

"That's fine. I have nothing to do today. Take the G-Class SUV. You may need the space." I love both my cars. My daddy always bought Mercedes-Benz, white with peanut butter interior. I have my daddy's favorite, the S500, and I decided to get the G-Class later. My dad would lose his mind, but he would be proud. I smile to myself.

"What are you smiling at?" Amelia asks.

"Oh, nothing. Just a memory I had of Dad."

Amelia comes to me and gives me a hug and for a moment I almost start crying at the sentimental moment.

"Sis, please be safe and I love you."

"I will and you have a safe day as well. Love ya." Amelia grabs the keys and leaves. She never understood why I had two cars, but now she understands. She is always borrowing one of them. I need to go to sleep, but I can't. The next best thing is coffee. This Keurig is the best thing they could have ever made. As I sit and enjoy my cup of hot coffee with cream and sugar, those girls start flashing in my mind again.

Page and I were just brainstorming last night about the missing girls. Officer Anthony Page is my partner. At first, I thought he hated me or hated the idea of being partners with a woman, but after time passed, he came to respect me. We always have each other's back. Lately though, he has been distant from me. I will have to call him to see how he is holding up, later. My mind drifts back to the missing girls.

They were placed strategically and methodically in areas where they would be found. Their heads lay on a blanket wrapped like a pillow. The blanket was made of cashmere and soft to the touch. Almost like a baby's blanket for comfort. It always looked like they were sleeping peacefully in the comfort and safety of their home. Their hair draped behind their ears with diamonds shining the brightest, even the prostitutes. Their latest farewell depicted a more intimate setting: beautiful exotic flowers surrounded them for the dedication of their souls and bodies. Large oak trees draped over them to protect them from harm; to protect them from shame. It's almost as if the killer wants them to be observed in the best light like all the squares in the city, beautiful and full of life with meaning to give to their onlookers.

Detective James Hall keeps blowing me off, but I am going to make him listen to me. I've never actually met the guy because when he shows up on scene, he is always sitting in the car. I always speak to his partner, Detective Kimberly Knight. She used to work in the same precinct as me, but adjoining beats. People always said we were a bit odd and kept to ourselves. That's probably why we got along so well. She is so nice, but very new to investigations. I wish they would pick me to go to the third floor. The third floor of Headquarters is the investigative wing. But I will wait my turn. It's coming.

Kim set up a meeting at The Grind, a local coffee hangout for cops, with me and Detective Hall. She is on the naïve side and really believes I have a theory to the killings. She wants to explain my theory to Hall and promised he will listen. This will be a waste of my time, but whatever, it's free coffee and I can head to the park and draw and read. That is my favorite thing to do in my free time. It brings me peace and sanity. I finally got back into dancing again; Afro dance to be exact. I stopped for a while, but I am starting to get back to my old self. I will never be the same, but I will grow to let go of the heartbreaking pain of my parents' death.

I find myself sitting around in the precinct, listening to the gossip. I learn that Detective Hall is an arrogant asshole, but damn good at his job. I can handle an asshole; my dad was the biggest of them all, but he always said, "Assholes have something to prove. Once you break through the outer layer of their defense wall, you will find that they are passionate, loving, and scared. They have something to prove. Find out what that is, and you will understand them more."

My phone rings... Kim's name pops up on the screen. I answer after two rings.

"We have another body..."

Chapter 2

Jason

There's nothing more relaxing than sitting on the balcony of my condo drinking a Tennessee Mule. The sun just set, and it blankets the city with an alluring ray of reds and purples. I hear the hustle and bustle of the downtown area. It can get pretty loud on weekends, but on weekdays it's a different feel. It's like the world slowing down and evaluating all the bad shit they did over the weekend. Me included. I find myself drifting into thoughts about life in general. I have everything I want: a nice house to come home to, money in my bank account, my baby sister is doing great in school, and I can get laid anytime I want. What else could I ask for?

I hear my alarm beep and I automatically grab my pistol sitting on the side table.

"Don't shoot, it's me, Dianella."

Allowing the air to leave my lungs, I physically calm down and place the gun back on the table. "What the hell, Dianella? I thought I told you to call before you just walk in here. I could have been fucking someone or, even worse, I could have shot you."

"I'm sorry. I was in the neighborhood and thought you would like to have something to eat. I know you work so much, and you are probably drowning your sorrows away with whiskey."

She is right. I haven't been eating like I should, but there is no way I am getting fat and I am a grown man; I can drink whatever the fuck I want. I wouldn't dare say that to her though.

"Yes, I could use something to eat with my main course." I throw her a smile and she roll her eyes.

"Whatever. I am the only one who will take care of you because you won't let anyone worthwhile in your life." She looks at me with those beautiful green eyes and she automatically reminds me of our mother. I push those thoughts out of my head.

"I haven't had anyone worthwhile in my life. Once I do, you will be the first to know."

"That's a load of crock. What about Jennifer or Jasmine? They were perfect and you just pushed them away. Ever since Big Mama died, you don't get attached to anyone. I want to be an auntie, you know."

She really knows how to punch directly in the gut. But she is right. No one is worthy of my time. Not right now anyway. I need to focus on these cases. Jennifer and Jasmine weren't good girls and they just didn't do it for me.

"And besides, you would probably confide in Ryan before you tell me anything."

"That's not true. I tell you everything." She throws her hand on her hip and looks at me with sarcasm.

"Oh, please. Anyways, come eat." She pulled out two dishes from the cabinet in the kitchen and set them on the island. I had an island made of refurbished wood to offset the décor in the kitchen and in the living room. My home is an open concept home because I want to be able to see everything at every angle. She then places a salad and steak on the plate. She knows me well. I don't eat a whole lot of carbs because I need to keep up with my physique.

I grab a bottle of wine from the wine cellar and two glasses. Red wine goes best with steak. I then pour her a glass and me a glass. Sometimes I have to remind myself that she is not a young kid driving me crazy anymore. She is a grown woman in college making a life for herself. She also works even though I told her she didn't have to work. She only shut me down and said, "We will always support each other; not you only supporting me." I have a much better respect for her because I know she is genuine. Jennifer and Jasmine were just after my money. They thought if they could fuck me then they were in. Even tried to get pregnant by me. I hate desperate women. It's gross and unattractive.

Dianella says the blessings and we dive right in. The steak is perfect—medium rare plus. Ruth's Chris really knows how to make a good steak. Dianella grows quiet after a while. She is content eating her steak and drinking her favorite wine, Apothic Red Blend. I found it cheap, but I will always keep a bottle for my baby sis. I prefer whiskey any day, but when I am around her, she makes me want to be better; do better.

After we eat our food, she cleans off the island, even though I tell her all the time she doesn't have to clean up behind me. I stopped arguing with her a long time ago. We then go back to the balcony and have a fresh cocktail. She has a mojito and I have a Tennessee Mule. For a while we just sit and listen to the night life. It becomes dark pretty quickly, but Broughton Street is still lit up with lights. For some reason I love people watching. It gives me peace.

"Are you happy, Jason?" The question comes out of nowhere and throws me off guard.

"What do you mean?"

"Are you happy how your life turned out? Do you aspire to want more?"

I sit silent for a while because I don't know how I want to answer the question. "Yes, I am happy. Are you happy?"

She looks at me with conflict and tension in her eyes. I've seen that type of conflict before. "I don't know. I mean, I'm glad I have you in my life, friends in my life, and doing well in school, but sometimes I miss having a mom and a dad. All of my friends have that. Well, except one, but for the most part they all have a mother who cares about them and a father who is supportive of their decisions. It's not fair that we don't have that." I can see her eyes get cloudy with tears and puffy. I grab her by the hand and pull her into my lap and hold her like I used to when she was just a kid.

"Dianella, I am your family. I am your father and your mother. I would never let anything happen to you, and you can always talk to me. Never assume that I am too busy for you, because I'm not. You are all I have, and I will never let you down." She places her head on my shoulder and I stroke her hair just like I used to when she was a kid. Sometimes she reminds me of her younger days when she felt insecure in life. I would calm her down when girls at school would pick on her for not having a mom or a dad.

She slowly gets up. "I'm sorry, I'm just a little emotional right now. One of the girls who was killed the other night was a friend of mine. Well, not a friend, but we were in the same class and we worked on projects together. It's just so sad how someone could be here one moment and gone the next. I just hope you find who keeps doing this."

That's all I needed to motivate me to solve this case. I wanted to protect my baby sister and all the other possible young victims out there totally oblivious of what danger lurks in the alleys or, how Savannahians say it, lanes.

"I promise I will find this person and bury them."

"I know you will." She gives me a big hug and I kiss her on her cheek. "I have to go. I have class early in the morning. I will see you tomorrow at the café."

"Okay." She walks out and I watch her on my camera system on my phone to make sure she gets in her car safely. I don't want to take any chances with my baby sister's life. I grab the glasses and walk inside the house. I close the door behind me and place the glasses in the dishwasher. I then start it and head to my room.

My room looks just like a bachelor's pad. Dianella wanted to decorate it for me, but I refused to let her in my room. It was off-limits to her. I didn't want her to smell or see any indiscretions in my bedroom. I wanted her to stay pure of heart. Wishful thinking on my part.

I turn on the TV, which is hanging on the wall opposite of my bed. I take my sweats off and get in bed. Then my phone lights up with a message.

> *Hey Detective Hall.*

> *Hey Knight, I keep telling you, you can call me Jason.*

> *I will never do that Detective Hall.*

> *Whatever, what do you want?*

> *Rude much?*

You texted me.

Anyways, I want you to meet Officer Lily Matthews.

Why?

I told you before, I think she could be a really good asset to the team.

We don't need anyone else on our team.

Yes, we do and get out of your ass.
She will be great for the team.
I've watched her work.
She is very good.

Fine, set up the meeting at The Grind. I can kill two birds with one stone.

Yeah, perfect. I think you would love her.

> *I only love my sister.*
> *Everyone else is*
> *chopped liver.*

> *Great, I'm glad I know where*
> *I stand with you.*

She doesn't text me back. Great, I just pissed her off.

> *Knight, I'm sorry.*
> *I didn't mean it that way.*

> *I know, you're just an ass*
> *who needs to get laid.*

She is right about that. I need pussy and I need it now. I think about calling Melissa. She is a fine piece of ass, but she doesn't do it for me either. Honestly, I don't feel like being bothered. I fall asleep because I am drunk and miserable. What seems like seconds later, my phone beeps.

"We have another body…"

Chapter 3

Lily

The sun hasn't quite risen to its full potential. The ground is still wet from the mist of the night. I've always loved early mornings to sit and relax in the park or take a long run on the Island.

"Lily, we need your help at the scene. Meet me at Crawford Square at Houston and E Perry Street," says Kim.

Shocked that she called me, I ask, "Are you sure? It's my day off..."

"Yes, we need your attention to detail and I already cleared it with Captain to allow the overtime. This is your chance to prove to them that you belong in this unit," says Kim.

She is a breath of fresh air. Always encouraging me to strive for my very best. I am absolutely terrified of failure, but...

"Okay, okay, okay. Let me throw something on. I will be there in twenty," I say.

Another girl, another life taken too soon. Sometimes I wonder what their last thoughts were. Were they scared; did they know it was coming; were they able to pray for their souls and loved ones? I used to believe in God, but sometimes I wonder why we go through so much pain in order to learn life's lessons. I started losing my faith after my parents died. The numbing pain was and still is too overwhelming. The number one question that could never be answered, WHY THEM AND NOT ME!

I remember the night I received the phone call. I was away for school in Atlanta, Georgia University. I was sitting in my dorm room studying for my clinical exams. I was in my second year of nursing school and all I thought about was achieving my goal; becoming a nurse and working back home in Savannah. The moment all my dreams were shattered is when I answered the phone.

"Hello," I said.

"Is this Lily Matthews, daughter of William and Yulanda Matthews?" the officer asked.

"Yes, this is she. Can I help you with something? Is everything okay?"

"Yes, there has been an accident and your parents and sister are at the hospital. We need you to come to Larson's Hospital."

That is all I remember of that night. I don't remember going to the hospital. I don't remember hearing the news of the death of my parents. I don't remember falling asleep. I don't remember anything. Only thing I remember is what people have told me since that night, that week, that month. I remember dropping out of school because I never went back. I stayed home to take care of my sister. There was no way I was letting the system take her from me. I was nineteen and she was sixteen. Amelia turned sixteen that night, when a drunk driver ran the red light hitting my parents' Mercedes S500 head-on. My parents were dead when they arrived at the hospital according to the police, but my sister was in critical condition. She was in and out of consciousness. Both her legs and her left arm were broken, so she was bound to a wheelchair for months. I had to be there to help her through therapy, but I could not remember any of it. It's still a blur; I only know what people have told me. I just want to be able to remember on my own.

While locking the doors and setting the alarm, I remember the day the lawyer sat me and my sister down. She explained to us that our parents left everything to us, and we would want for nothing. There was enough for the house, the bills, Amelia's schooling, my schooling…if I went back. I chose to work because I was slipping into depression and I had to get my aunt Beverly off my back. She wanted me and Amelia to sell the house and live with her in Atlanta, but I absolutely will never get rid of my parents' house. My daddy built this house from the ground up. He always said, "Build a sturdy foundation and the rest is easy." My goodness, I miss him so much. I was always a daddy's girl. Amelia was always close to our mom. I just like getting my hands dirty while Amelia played with Barbie dolls. I was always outside with Daddy, building things, shooting in the woods, rock climbing, and anything else related to outdoors.

Sometimes I wonder if I didn't answer the phone, would my parents be still alive? Would I have finished school?

I pulled up in my white Mercedes S500 with peanut butter interior, just like Daddy's. I shouldn't drive my car to this type of environment, but I don't want to drive my marked unit. Besides, it's my day off and I still want to go to Forsyth Park once I leave here.

As I get out of the car, I see Kim. That uniform does her no justice. She is tall like me at five-foot-seven, with beautiful brown wavy hair, and I always laugh at her because she never knows what to do with her hair. She has striking blue eyes and skin the color of hot creamy caramel with tiny freckles on her cheeks. I've never seen eyes like hers on a Black woman. As I walk up to her, I see a stunning man standing next to her. Their backs are toward me. My gosh he is gorgeous. He appears to be six-foot-two with brown hair, the color of hot mocha flared with excitement, clean cut with no facial hair. His arms are the size of my thighs and an ass fit for a god. That suit fits him so well, navy blue, as if it was tailored specifically for him. He looks like a runway model. If I could just see his eyes. Right on cue, as he looks away from the crime scene, our eyes meet. I am immediately pulled into a trance. His eyes are the color of a rain forest in the middle of spring, bright and purposeful. His demeanor has the will to solve anything; a desire to fulfill excellence in his goal. He has the skin color of a desert storm, very tanned. I would love to see what's underneath that suit. Jesus, my panties are soaked. How long has it been? My gosh, it's been a long time since my last one-night stand. Now that I think about it, it was absolutely awful. I was bored out of my mind. I had to go home and use Becky to get me right after that horrible night with what's-his-name...

"Lily, over here. I want you to meet Detective Jason Hall. He is the lead investigator of these cases. Detective Hall, this is Officer Lily Matthews," Kim says. Detective Hall is absolutely gorgeous. He just stands there without saying anything as if he is in deep thought, so I speak first.

"Hi, it is nice to meet you. I hate that it's under these circumstances, but nonetheless, it's a pleasure," I say. His eyes are so intense, like he is trying to communicate with me with just a look. He makes me feel vulnerable, but yet desired and powerful. He looks at me as if he knows all my secrets and scary moments. I feel like I want to breathe the same air as he does, touch his powerful hands.

"I am here to observe and learn as much as possible," I say.

"According to Detective Knight, I am the one who needs to learn from you," he says. "Apparently, you have a keen eye for detail, so be my guest; teach me something I already don't know."

"Okay," I say, ignoring the smart-ass comment he just made. What an asshole. He must not know who he talking to. He needs me, not the other way around. But I will play this game because I want to learn. Therefore, I suck up my pride, sign into the evidence sheet log with the street officer and start observing the area. I never treat the crime scene as a crime scene. I treat it like I am in my room or screened-in porch, drawing every feeling and detail of the earth. I become one with the green grass, let the flowing trees whisper to me all their fears, and let the flowers sing their wants and desires from the mockingbirds and hummingbirds.

All the victims have been placed in the Historic Downtown area for a reason. Each body found in a different square. History has it each square was planned and named before it was built. The squares and parks of Savannah are the community's most beloved icons. Originally designed with twenty-four squares, twenty-two remain today to be enjoyed by the millions who grace their grassy utopias every year including me. I love sitting in the squares and drawing the tourists coming and going, taking pictures, and socializing. People love coming to Savannah because it holds so much history. As I walk around, I try to step into the mind of this serial killer. I believe he chose these areas because of the uniqueness of each square. I believe each of the victims has a personal connection to the squares where they've been laid to rest for the final time. Once again, he laid his victim down as if she was sleeping, carefully tucking her hair behind her ear. She has diamonds in her ears, a half carat to be exact. Daddy bought a pair for my sister for her sixteenth birthday as he did mine. He always said a woman should own a pair of diamonds, and a man should buy them for us. He said he would be that man.

I continue to observe the area. I'm in my element. I'm talking to myself, but out loud. Kim and Detective Hall are following close behind recording the details.

"She is athletic, strong legs. She has tights on, black to be exact, but a bright lime green tank on. Her skin is smooth, yet olive due to the lividity setting in. Her hair is long and wavy and carefully kept like the others. She reminds me of a dancer or a gymnast. She is missing her phone, bag, purse, keys, anything that may belong to her. Kim, have the officers check all the trash cans in the area; her belongings will be in there." I continue to observe the area. "She was killed somewhere else and placed here. Somewhere where he can spend time with his victim. He admires his victim. He wants her to be trusting of him up to the very moment he takes that last breath from her. He cares about her and her image. He does not want anyone to see her in a bad light. He loves her, almost obsessed with her. I do not believe the women he is killing are the woman he wants. I think he wants his true love to notice him. He sees his real obsession every day, but she does not see him. Not the same way he sees her. He is going to continue to kill until she notices him. There are twenty-two squares and now five victims..."

"Five victims?" asks Detective Hall.

"Yes, if you go back to the first two bodies you found. They were prostitutes, but they were placed in similar areas and laid to rest the same way. This guy started out with women who no one gave a damn about. Since no one noticed anything, he moved to women who had purpose, who resembled his true love, the real victim in his eyes."

"Look, I took pictures of all the scenes. You tell me that I am wrong."

"That's against policy," Detective Hall says under clenched teeth.

"It may be against policy, but I am right."

19

"Detective Knight, we found the victim's gym bag with all her belongings in the trash can over here," says one of the street officers. I look up because I recognize the voice.

The street officer is Officer Page. "Hey, Page, I didn't know you were working today." We were both scheduled off today.

"Yeah, I am working overtime to purchase a new camera. What about you, why are you working today?" Officer Page asks.

"Oh, yes. I received a call to help with the case. Apparently, I have a keen eye for details. Who knew." I laugh to myself. "I have to get back to work, but we will catch up sometime." As I start to turn around, it seems that Page wants to say more, but doesn't. I think he wasn't expecting me there. I start to walk toward Kim and Detective Hall, overhearing their conversation.

"Just listen to her; she knows what she is talking about. I asked for her to work with us on this case and Captain Hill said it was okay," says Kim.

"You did what?" Detective Hall says furiously. He looks at Kim with disdain in his eyes. Boy, he is furious right now, but yet so alluring.

Catching both of them off guard, I say, "I know where I am not wanted, and I have other shit to be worried about than stroking someone's ego. Kim, if you need me, I will be at my usual place. Other than that, don't bother calling me again. I obviously don't need to be here."

I start walking back to my car. Kim runs up to me and says, "Ignore him. He knows you gave more information to go on than he ever had to work with. Please come back. For me. I need you."

"I will help you, Kim, but I do not need the extra drama in my life. I already have enough on my plate. He is an arrogant ass-hole who is full of shit. If he wants me to help, then he needs to ask for my help; until then, he can go to hell. I will see you tomorrow at the range."

"Okay, I will talk with him. Until then, if you have anything else to add, please call me day or night. I will listen. He is a good person, you know. He just has to get to know you."

"Okay, whatever, Kim. See you tomorrow."

I then leave. I notice Detective Hall looking at my car as I drive away…

Chapter 4

Jason

I drive to Tybee Island to clear my head. I love to feel the cold waves crashing against my legs, and the sand between my toes. I park my car near the pier. As I get out of my car and walk to the beach, I hear the laughs of happy children and the seagulls squawking in the distance. I smell the salt from throughout the ocean and the sunscreen from those wary of the sun. I see the boats sailing and shipping containers in the distance and the never-ending solid horizon, and the sun sets into the distance. I can taste the salt as the waves splash against my legs.

Officer Matthews is unbelievably gorgeous, and she doesn't even realize it. Most women in her caliber know they are hot, and it makes them pains in the ass with an even more entitled attitude than the average woman, but not Matthews. She carries herself with personality and intelligence, shy but tough. She will stand up for herself. She certainly put me in my place.

The second she stepped out of that S500, I knew I wanted to fuck her. My dick was so hard, I could barely control myself. Her skin is the color of creamy milk chocolate with a hint of caramel delight. There is no need for makeup because she is already stunning without it. Her hair flowed in the wind with never-ending waves. And those eyes, my god those eyes…hazel with a hint of green. I would love to see those legs pushed back over my shoulders while I ram my hard, thick dick inside that pussy. I just want to see if it's pink and perky or caramel and strong.

Black women have always turned me on. A Black woman is a complex and intricate being. As a white man, I find an array of Black women beautiful. She could be light-skinned, dark-skinned, slim, curvy, tall, short, have straight or curly hair, and it doesn't matter; she is beautiful regardless. Matthews is light-skinned, curvy, tall, and has long, natural, wavy hair with stunning hazel eyes. What's not to love.

I think I get my love for Black women from my adoptive mother, Allison Taylor, known as Big Mama. I was a complete terror, but she always prayed for my soul. She kept me safe and if it wasn't for her and my sister, Dianella, I wouldn't be here today. I was headed down a spiraling dark tunnel, getting into trouble with the law just about every night. I never thought in a million years I would become a police officer, let alone a detective. My birth mother was a crack addict. She was always trying to find her next fix. She wasn't always like this. My father, Johnathan Hall, left us when I was eight years old. Dianella was only three years old. She doesn't remember our parents and she doesn't want to remember. Dianella attends nursing school and business school at Georgia College. She is doing very well, and I am her number one fan when it comes to her achievements. Big Mama made sure we got a good education no matter what. She wanted us to understand that our past does not dictate our future; it just makes us strong and strive to overcome obstacles.

As I watch Matthews drive away, I know I want to get to know her better. Don't get me wrong, this case is priority, but what's wrong with mixing work with pleasure? Two small children interrupt my guttered mind while laughing at the waves destroying their creation with the sand. They are so innocent at that age. Just like the girls who are turning up dead all over the downtown area of Savannah. I looked at the pictures Matthews took, and she is right, they are all connected. I hate that she is right, but needless to say, she is. I never even looked into the prostitution side of these killings. I wrote them off as street walkers and they had it coming. I think that is why I yelled at Matthews. I didn't want her to be right. I really need to apologize to her. If she listens to me again. I will get Knight to set up a meeting with her again at my business, The Grind.

No one knows that I am part owner of the most popular coffee shop in the downtown area and I would like to keep it that way. The only people who know are Detective Knight and my best friend, Ryan Taylor. He made some pretty sweet investments for me and I hit big. I am now a multimillionaire and really don't have to work, but I love what I do. I love the business I built from the ground up. My sister is the other partner in The Grind. Everyone knows her because she is a people person. She is the face of the company while I supply the funding. I like it that way better.

While walking back to my car, I receive a text.

> *Jason meet me at the Roof Top for drinks tonight. And I don't want to hear no.*

I reply back to Ryan.

> *I guess I will see you at nine.*

Ryan and I arrive at the Roof Top and follow the sound of live music to the rooftop, where you will discover something surprising—breathtaking views of the Savannah River and Historic District at one of the best bars in Savannah. I enjoy indulging in a tempting selection of tapas, sip a handcrafted cocktail, and let my cares sail beyond the river. My favorite poison is a Tennessee Mule with Jack Daniel's whiskey and a splash of ginger beer. I will drink a neat whiskey every now and then, but when I need to blow off some steam, I always revert to the Tennessee Mule. It's refreshing and it gets me in the mood for an easy lay. I need something to take the edge off, take my mind off Matthews.

Ryan and I grab a table outside near the blazing fire. We lounge around, watching all the free pussy come and go. I haven't found my prey just yet, but she will walk through that door any second now. Ryan, on the other hand, will fuck anything with two legs. I need someone who has a brain, who can hold a conversation before I fuck her. I don't want to marry the chick, but at least be on my level.

As we listen to the band play, in walks two chicks with the tightest short dresses in the bar. Both are tall and stunning, with curves out of this world, and then as one of them turns around, I notice who they are… Knight and Matthews. Fuck, I have to sit up in my seat to get a closer look. Matthews just knocked the breath right out of me. She is one fine piece of ass. Knight is not half bad either, but she is not my type and she is my partner for god's sake. But I know she is Ryan's type. That damn uniform does her no justice. I had no idea she looked like that underneath. I punch Ryan in the arm to get his attention.

"Aw, that shit hurt…"

"Six o'clock at the bar. I need your back, bro." He walks away from the chick he was talking to and looks where I am looking.

"Bro, we got this."

Knight is searching for a table to sit at when she notices me and Ryan. She waves and starts walking toward us. Matthews is still at the bar getting their drinks when a dude walks up to her. Assuming he is offering to buy her drink, I get up immediately and stalk over to her. I grab her by the waist and ask, "Did you miss me?" She is getting ready to turn around and hit me in the face when she stops in her tracks and stares into my eyes. God, she is absolutely stunning. Her hair down her back, lip gloss on her lips, and a black silk dress that probably cost more than her salary, snug around her hips. The guy gets the hint and starts hunting elsewhere.

"Can I help you?" she asks, turning back toward the bar.

Yes, you can, you can bend over this counter right now and let me fuck that pretty little ass of yours.

"Yes, I would love for us to start over. Hi, my name is Jason. What's yours?"

"My name is Lily. It's a pleasure to meet you." What a beautiful name. It really fits her.

"We have a table outside near the fire if you would like to join us." She looks at the area that I am referring to and find Knight and Ryan already engaging in conversation.

"I guess I really don't have a choice. Okay, just let me get these drinks and I will be right over."

"I will help you…"

"No, it's okay. I got it. Thanks though."

She must really not know who I am. I will never allow a woman to pay for her own drink especially if I know she doesn't make a whole lot.

"Paul, put those drinks on my tab and anything else the ladies wish to order. Thanks, bro."

"Just like that, hon… Does that work for all the ladies?"

"Only the ones I like and respect…" I get a smile out her for that one. Boy, her smile is mesmerizing. Perfect lips, perfect teeth, with a little dimple in the left cheek. Once she gets the drinks, I take one from her hand and guide her to our seats. As she sits down, the breeze runs across her delicate skin, blowing her hair across her face and into my senses. She smells like a fresh orchard of apples blossoming in the springtime. I can smell her hair all day every day and will never get tired of it.

"Thanks, Hall, for getting my drink. I appreciate it."

"My pleasure, Knight. What brings you out tonight? I've never seen you here before," I ask Lily.

Her phone pings and she pick it up before she answers the question. After reading the text and responding she looks up at me with an annoyed look on her face. Whatever the text was has changed her attitude slightly, but she bounces back within seconds as if it never even bothered her.

"Kim dragged me out of my house and refused to leave until I gave in. You got to love your friends. I am more of a stay at home and drink a glass of wine on my back porch kind of girl. I really do not like crowded places, which is why we are here. I love the atmosphere here more so than any of the other clubs in City Market."

My kind of girl. I'd rather be laid up on my balcony watching the night life more than experiencing it on my own. This is Ryan's scene.

"Same here. Rather be home, but Ryan insisted I come out. I'm glad I did." Wow, watching her blush and show a little hint of vulnerability is so cute.

"So, I wanted to talk with you about the case…"

"No talking about work tonight. We have the night off to relax and live in the moment. If you absolutely have to talk about the case, we can chat tomorrow at The Grind. What do you say?"

"I love The Grind. That's my favorite spot. I love the coffee and the owner is amazing. She is so smart and loveable. She reminds me of my sister."

I love the way she is so passionate about something. She lights up with excitement. Who knew my business was her favorite spot to hang out? But, now that I think about it, I did see her there one time. I just didn't pay attention.

"Oh, I'm sorry, I am rambling on and did not answer you. Yes, I would love to meet you for coffee tomorrow to go over the case."

"No need to apologize. It's my favorite spot too. I've just been busy."

"Oh, I understand."

"So, you have a sister..."

"Yes, her name is Amelia." Dianella mentioned an Amelia a while back, but I was so busy I forgot about it.

"That's a beautiful name."

"After our parents died, Amelia and I became very close. She means everything to me."

"I'm sorry for your loss."

"No need, it was a long time ago."

"Still, I understand the loss of a parent; it's not easy."

"Wow, you lost your parents also? I had no idea. I am sorry to hear that as well. I guess you do understand. Most people say they do, but really don't. I wish people would just leave me alone."

"It gets better, just give it time."

"I hope so. Enough about that. What do you like to do for fun?" she asks.

"Work, play, and fuck really hard." I know that was blunt, but I am a straight-up blunt person.

"Getting straight to the point," she says with no reaction at all. Impressive.

"What do you like to do for fun?" I challenge her.

"Well, I love to draw, read, relax on my back porch, and fuck hard."

Now, that surprises the fuck out of me. I did not see that coming. This woman amazes me beyond my wildest dreams. My dick just got harder than I could ever imagine. I am about to bust right out of my jeans. God, I want to take her right now, lifting that silk dress above her ass, letting her long legs straddle my hips as I am ramming into that tight pussy of hers. I just want a little taste. God, now she is biting that lower lip of hers, so plump and juicy. She is driving me wild and she doesn't even realize it. Focus, Jason, focus.

"I also enjoy rock climbing, hiking, and performance shooting. I thought about joining SWAT but decided not to. I prefer drawing more so than chasing idiots." She then takes a small sip of her cabernet. Watching her sip her wine is taking me into bliss. I need to release now. Control yourself, Jason.

"Hey, Lily. Do you want to walk to City Market? It's a beautiful night and they have live music in the square," Kim says, breaking my train of thought.

"That's a good idea. Let's get out of here," I say, before I explode. I need to walk around to get my composure back. "Ryan, Lily, what do you say?"

"Sounds good," Lily says.

"Let's do this, bro," Ryan says.

I go to pay the tab and we then leave the bar, leaving a one-hundred-dollar tip. These guys always take care of me, so I take care of them. Walking down Bay Street toward City Market gives me the calming I need. Lily has become my own brand of heroine. Watching her walk from behind gives life a whole new purpose. Watching her thick hips sway from side to side as if she is the only one on a runway. The moon's delicate light turns the world aflame with silver as she walks. She needs no fancy clothes to look good even though that dress is mind-blowing. She is smart in the head, and courageous in the heart, confident in herself, and compassionate in her thoughts. She is independent and able, strong and graceful. Little does she know, I live right in the heart of downtown, my loft overlooking the hustle and bustle of nightlife. She will be mine, but not tonight. I will wait, but our time is coming.

The music fills the air, and tourists and locals dance in Ellis Square, where the heart of City Market is surrounded by tall historic hotels, lofts, boutiques, and bars. Ryan grabs Knight and starts swaying to the music, but that is not what takes my breath away. Lily closes her eyes and gracefully glides in the middle of the square. She is drifting to the music, a song so seductive, every man in a hundred-foot radius is getting a hard-on just watching her. I notice a figure in the dark of the alley staring in our direction, but I am too hypnotized to really give a damn. I've got to have her. I need to be inside of her. I walk up behind her and reach my muscular arms around her waist. I notice a small jolt, but so small no one else would notice. I feel her pulse racing as I guide my hands down her waist. She continues to sway to the music even when it changes tempo. We are in our own world, just the two of us making love to the music in our heads. I whisper in her ear, "Come to my loft."

"I can't leave Kim; we rode together," she says.

"She is in good hands. I trust Ryan with my life. Besides, they look like they are in their own world." She pulls away and calls out to Kim to come over. They whisper something to each other, and she walks away and heads toward me.

"Sure, I will come with you, but promise me one thing?" she says.

"Anything…"

"Promise me you will never fall in love with me."

Without even thinking, I utter the words she wants to hear even though I am pretty sure I won't break them. "I promise." Crossing my heart with my finger.

We then head a block over to Broughton Street. It comes back to me that the dark figure I saw earlier is not there anymore. Oh, well.

"I live above Starbucks in a small loft I renovated."

"Really, the noise doesn't bother you?" she asks.

"No, I could never sleep, so most of the time I sit on my balcony and watch the chaos around me. It's therapeutic in a way. It helps me think."

We walk up to the side door to my loft. I place my finger on the keypad. It grants me entrance to the elevator. I then push "penthouse," which is on the top floor of the building. As the doors open to my home, Lily's eyes light up. Walking into an open floor plan with tall, vaulted ceilings, I have an eighty-inch Samsung HDTV on the wall. It's the first thing you see when you walk into my loft. To the right I have my chocolate brown leather sofa with accent chairs to complement the living area. The living area overlooks the downtown area. You can see the Talmadge Bridge from my balcony. To the left, I have my kitchen settled in the corner, open concept with a large island with barstools lined up to it. I have a large restaurant-size fridge that Anna keeps stocked for me. She is my maid/cook/butler whatever I need. She is a godsend. I would not survive without her. Her words, not mine.

"Lily, would you like a glass of wine?"

"Sure... Cab..."

"I know. Remember, I'm very observant."

"Thank you, but you don't know that I like a splash of Sweet Bitch in my cabernet sauvignon. It's the perfect seduction in my mouth," she says.

"Really, I will have to try that."

"So, Jason, tell me about your family."

"You really want to hear about my family?"

"Yes, I am interested in hearing about your family."

She looks at me with those beautiful hazel eyes and I just fall apart. I grab her glass from her hand and place it on the counter. I then lift her up and place her on the island. She looks down at me with those baby doe eyes. She circles her legs around my waist and pulls me closer with her heels. I take a deep breath and inhale her perfume which complements her natural scent so well. With one hand I lift her dress up and feel her ass in my palm while kissing her neck. I suck and tug on her delicate skin just behind her ear. I use my hands to explore the rest of her body, reaching for her long curly hair. Her hair is so soft and mesmerizing. I pick her up and head for my bedroom. As I lay her down on the bed...my phone beeps.

Another body found in Wright Square.

All hands on deck...

Chapter 5

Lily

Once Jason receives the page, we compose ourselves and head to the Whittaker Street garage so I can get my car. Thank goodness I keep a change of clothes in all my vehicles. I change in the car and head to the scene, one block south of the garage. I didn't want to walk because I didn't want anyone to think I was out partying or hanging out with Jason. All I can think about is him grabbing me, aggressively kissing my neck and on the verge of fucking my brains out. God, we were so close. I can still feel his lips on my neck, his hands exploring my body, his hard chest grazing my nipples, making them hard as pebbles. We were so close. I so need Becky right now.

I arrive on scene and there are people everywhere, news crew, police officers, tourist, locals. It's a madhouse. I walk toward the body when Kim grabs my hand and pulls me toward her.

"SOOO…tell me what happened?" Kim asks.

"Nothing happened."

"Seriously, you aren't going to give me anything?" she asks.

"Nothing happened. We had a drink and talked. Then we received the call for this body. Now I am here, the end."

"Fine, don't share."

"What's going on with you and Ryan?" I ask.

"The man is a sex god. He fucked me into the middle of next week. We meet up again for a date tomorrow, that is if we get home at a decent time tonight," she says.

"TMI, Kim, TMI." I start going into my zone, observing the scene. I speak loud enough for Kim to hear me. Each square is unique in its appearance, but what I've found are the lily pad-like plants. Now that I think about it, all the bodies are found near exotic plants. This shows me that the killer thinks his victims are exotic or should be exotic. He finds them sexy in appearance, but yet sexy in intelligence. Again, the victim's head lies on a blanket tucked under her head like a pillow, hair swept behind her ear to show off her diamond earrings. This time, her stuff is scattered around her. She has bruising on her legs and arms as if she fought back. She didn't know him, nor did she want to go anywhere with him. This killing is more aggressive than the other five deaths. I notice that there is something underneath her nails, possibly skin from her assailant. Kim is following me and recording me. She directs forensics to take samples and pictures of all the evidence. I then start walking around the square. This square is alarming compared to the other squares because it is near the school board, with a private school on the other side;

each building has cameras. I see a piece of paper folded up on the ground. It seems out of place, so I put my gloves on and pick it up. I unfold the paper, which has a poem or something written on it.

I read it out loud,

"Tonight, the city is ours, it's true
A dreamland created for just me and you
There will be something sweet as pie
Where you find something good to eat for you and I
As we savor our time much long overdue."

"It sounds like a clue to something," says Hall.

"It could be nothing," I say. "Did you find any notes at any of the other squares where the girls were left?"

"No, but we weren't looking either."

Frustrated, I call out to Kim. "Kim, this is what I need: access to all of the cameras in this area, a rush on all DNA testing, and get me a background of all the victims. These girls are related in some way; we just need to figure it out. And have one of the officers come with me so we can re-canvass the other scenes. We missed something. I just have a gut feeling. Thanks, Kim. Appreciate your assistance in this." My phone pings, and I receive another text from Page.

Is everything okay?

Yes, why?

You haven't come to
work in a while.
Just checking on you.

I'm good. Working
a case with the
Homicide Unit.

The missing girls case?

Yeah, actually I am on a
scene now. Can I text you
back later? Detective Hall
is a dick sometimes.

Yeah, sure. Stay focused.
This is your chance to show
them who you really are. Twyl.

Okay, and thanks for the
confidence boost.

Of course.

As I put my phone back in the pocket, I notice Jason watching and observing me. I can never tell what he is thinking. He always has this stoic look. I find it methodically challenging; strikingly sexy, and mysteriously charming. He may be stone hard in public, but in the bedroom…my god, he could fuck me right here, right now, and I wouldn't even care. My panties are dripping wet right now just thinking about his lips on my pussy, sucking on my clit, making me reach a high I never have before.

Interrupting my train of thought, Jason comes up to me and taps me on the shoulder.

"Detective Matthews." Now we are back to formalities. I don't mind, work is work and play is play. I don't need all these people in my business, and I don't want people thinking I fucked my way to the top. I want people to see my talent, my dedication, and my strengths.

"Yes, Detective Hall. How can I help you?"

"If you don't mind coming to the office to help with this case, we really could use your assistance. I also want to apologize for my behavior before. You deserve respect from me, and I know you didn't realize that taking pictures of the scenes on your personal phone was against policy." What an apology. I never thought in a million years I would hear those words come from this man…the sky must be falling.

I suck my pride in without plastering a grin on my face, but I am laughing inside.

"Thank you, and yes, I will head over to the office as soon as I am done here. I want to canvass the other scenes again as well to see if we missed anything. This scene had more than we bargained for."

"What else do you see?"

"I want to check the trash cans. Since her belongings are scattered around her, I want to see if he left a present for us in the trash." I then start checking the trash cans. When I come to the last one, I start taking things out, such as beer bottles, soda cans, old food containers, clothing, and then…

"Look. Detective Knight and Hall, come here."

I lift up six different photos of our victims. All unique in a way. The first two are of the prostitutes. I figure they are part of his prize possessions. These pics are of them dressed in wedding gowns with makeup and jewelry on. The necklace is made of black pearls, earrings of pure diamonds, and a wedding band fit for a queen. They all look happy and willing to take the photos. This is the connection.

"The suspect is an artist, photographer, or designer. He wants the girls at their best, but how do they come to him willingly?"

"What about an ad online or the newspaper?" Kim suggests. "Believe it or not, we are in a city where there are a lot of destination weddings. Advertisement would be ideal to get tourists and brides here for their weddings. They are having their weddings in these very squares, and most of them are in Forsyth Park. What if he is targeting these areas based on destination weddings?"

"Detective Knight, you are on to something. But I still think he is trying to impress someone. Someone who likes to watch the weddings maybe or someone who coordinates the weddings. Nevertheless, we need to figure this out before there is another killing. He is not killing them in the squares, he is taking them somewhere else to kill them and then dumping them in the squares. Once we find out who he really is passionate about, then we will find our killer. We have to find her before he makes his move," I say.

We let the Forensics Unit complete their job and then the three of us head back to the office. I need a coffee now. It looks like it will be a long night.

Arriving in separate vehicles, Jason, Kim, and I walk up to the Homicide Unit. There is a flat-screen TV on one of the walls and a clear dry erase board on the opposite wall. An executive board table sits in the middle of the room with leather chairs surrounding the table. A Keurig sits on the wet bar counter perpendicular to the flat-screen TV. The way the room is set up represents an interactive briefing, collaborative and motivational. The Homicide Unit has all the newest technology and equipment to help solve cases along with the Forensics Unit. The first place I head for is the Keurig machine. They even have real creamer and not that powered stuff, and real sugar.

"Anyone want a cup?"

"Absolutely," they say in unison.

"I want mine black, please," says Jason.

"And I want mine with cream and sugar," says Kim. "There is no other way to drink coffee."

Jason starts laughing at Kim while I prepare the coffee. "I will have to agree with Kim. I love my coffee with cream and sugar as well, but very strong. The Grind makes the best coffee. I wish they were open right now." I notice Kim and Jason exchange a look, but it was so quick I wonder if I'm seeing things. Kim hangs up pics of the six women we found so far. She also pulls up their background history, family history, and pictures of the scenes. I look at each victim's background history. As I am comparing the six, I notice something identical with all victims.

"Did you know that all the girls attended Georgia College and were all foster kids?"

"No, we did not put that together until now. I've been waiting on the workup for a while. Our SARIC unit is understaffed and overworked," says Kim.

"Kim wasn't lying; you are great with detail and observation. We've been working this case for three weeks and did not come this far until now," says Jason.

"What foster home did they come from?" I ask.

"It looks like they all came from Greenbriar. The first victim, Stacy, lost both of her parents in a car accident. She and her sister were placed in foster care because they had no other family. She later became a street walker and ended up dropping out of college. The second victim, Charisma, lost her entire family in a car accident. She also dropped out of college due to overwhelming substance abuse. She became a street walker. Victims three through six all attended Georgia College as well, but they are remarkably smart. They all have 4.0 GPAs and were involved in extracurricular activities, such as sports, dance, gymnastics. They were foster kids because of the death of their parents, but were all adopted by loving families, which is why they are thriving so well."

I can feel myself get extremely hot, like overwhelming heat starting from my feet and rising to my head. I can't breathe; I am becoming dizzy. I step back a little, losing my balance. I start to fall.

Chapter 6

Lily

"**L**ily… Lily?" I hear Jason calling my name. Where am I? I open my eyes and find Jason, Kim, and EMS standing over me. I find my voice.

"What happened?"

"You fainted after looking at the backgrounds of the victims."

I scramble to my feet and back myself to the corner of the room. "I need to find my sister."

"Why?" says Kim.

"She may be the next victim."

"What the fuck are you talking about?" asks Jason.

"All these girls...they...they...look just like my sister. They remind me of us."

"Here, sit down, Lily. Here is a glass of water. Now start from the beginning. Why do you think your sister is in trouble?" Kim asks.

I take out a picture of me and my sister that I keep in my wallet.

"Here, look at the picture. You tell me what you see."

"I see a beautiful young woman with long, wavy hair, hazel brown eyes like yours, and beautiful light brown skin..."

"What you don't see is that my sister went into foster care at the age of sixteen. I had to go through the court system to get custody of her. Our parents died in a car accident by a drunk driver on my sister's sixteenth birthday. She was in the vehicle as well. She suffered broken bones and was bound to a wheelchair. I can't understand why I am remembering all this. I lost my memory of the whole incident because my doctor says I suffered from mild amnesia. Once I won custody of my sister, she came to live with me. I dropped out of college to raise her. She is currently attending Georgia College's Nursing Program. She is doing very well. What I am trying to say is, my sister went to Greenbriar for a couple of weeks because we lost both our parents and I had to prove that I was fit enough to take care of her. My sister has the same background as these young ladies. I need to find her." I start to get up and I fall right back down, overwhelmed with dizziness.

"You aren't going anywhere. We will send a car out to the school to find your sister," Jason demands.

"No, what time is it?" I ask.

"Two in the morning," Kim announces.

"She should be home by now. She left dance class at midnight."
I check my phone to see if the alarm has been turned off. It
hasn't. "She hasn't made it home. I have an app on my phone
to find her." I search my app and notice that it has been turned
off. "No, no, no…this can't be happening." I start panicking.

"What is it?" Jason asks.

"Her app has been turned off or disabled. I can't find my sister."

"Kim, get with Forensics. They will be able to find where her
last known location is by researching the app. Also, call my sister and find out where she is. Dianella should be with Amelia."

"Hold on, how do you know my sister? I never showed you the
picture. I only spoke about her."

"She is best friends with my sister. She comes by The Grind all
the time."

"The Grind? How do you know this? I can't think right now. I
need to process all this. It's too much. I need to find my sister.
NOW." I get up again and dial my sister's number. Then I head
for the door.

"If you insist on finding your sister, I am going with you and you
are not stopping me." Jason calls his sister while walking with
me to my car. Apparently, she does not answer the first time,

because he tries again. He grabs my keys and heads for the driver's side.

"What are you doing?"

"I told you, you're not driving anywhere in your condition. If you insist on putting yourself in danger, then I will make you stay at the office. Now, get your ass in the car or drag your ass upstairs and stay put. Those are your two options."

I pout, contemplating if I should fight him on this. I really don't have the energy or the time to argue with him right now. I get in the passenger seat and keep my mouth shut. All of two minutes that is.

"How do you know my sister?" I ask.

"I don't know her."

"Don't play games with me. Tell me how you know my fucking sister, or I am jumping out this fucking car right now."

"Your sister comes to my coffee shop all the time. She became best friends with my sister about a year ago. I never put the two together until now. Dianella started pulling away from me about a year ago because our parents died as well. When she met Amelia, she became alive again. I got my sister back. I never questioned her friendship because I didn't want to lose my sister."

"This is crazy. My sister and I have always been very close. We talk about everything. Why wouldn't she tell me about Dianella? Hell, I even go to the coffee shop as well. But you know what? I never went to The Grind with my sister. I always pick up a to-go order or she would do the same for me."

"Wow, all this time our sisters were best friends and we never knew it or discovered it on our own. What a coincidence."

"Hold on, wait a minute. You own The Grind?"

"Yes, I own it with my sister, Dianella. She runs the day-to-day activities. I manage the books and more behind the scenes. I don't want people to know I own the business because of my position on the department."

"Wow, I would have never guessed." I want to know more about this mystery man. But I need to put that on the back burner. I need to first find my sister and do my damn job. My phone rings and I almost lose my shit trying to answer the damn phone.

"Amelia, is this you?" I never looked at the caller ID.

"Yes, sis. Is everything okay? I am at a friend's house."

"Tell me the address. I am heading over right now."

"Sixty-two Redrock Circle."

"Okay, don't leave; we are on our way."

"Yes, okay. But you are scaring me."

"I will explain everything to you when I get there." I start to put the address in the GPS when Jason stops me. I look at him, waiting for him to explain.

"I know where the address is. It's my parents' house. She will not be able to get a signal in that area because they are just now putting in cell towers."

Dumbfounded, I just sit and listen. What the fuck is going on? I put my head in the palms of my hands and rock back and forth. About fifteen minutes later we arrive at this beautiful two-story home overlooking a private lake. It's more of an estate than a single-family home. It has a six-car garage, fully bricked, with tall pillars on the front porch. There is a driveway that leads up to each of the garage doors. It's absolutely breathtaking. Jason pulls up to the front porch. He then gets out of the car. I stay seated unable to move. I feel paralyzed with overwhelming grief, anger, sadness, cluelessness, and so on…

"Are you coming?" he asks.

I can't move; I can't breathe. He walks over to my side of the car, opens the door, and swings my legs out the door. He places his hands on my thighs and tells me to breathe.

"Lily, follow my breathing. I need you to look into my eyes and follow exactly what I am doing."

I look into those beautiful eyes full of hope, fear, and strength. He takes a deep breath and then lets out a small breath. I follow his lead. I start to calm down with just looking into his eyes. I've never felt so weak and strong at the same time. I feel weak because I am depending on a man for strength. I feel strong because I am depending on this man for strength. I place my hands in his and squeeze as I follow his breathing. He then grabs my hands and guides me out of the car.

"You can do this. You must be strong for your sister. She needs you right now. We will talk about what happened at the office later, but for now you need to be strong. Can you do that for me?"

I will follow this man to the moon and haven't even felt him inside of me.

"Yes, I can do this." I stand up and close the car door. I take a deep breath and follow him into his childhood home. It has a grand entrance with a staircase on both sides of the foyer. It has a chandler that lights up the room. I look up and see my sister standing at the top of the stairs with Dianella. I run up the stairs and grab my sister and wrap my arms around her so tight. I don't think I can let go of her. I start to cry all over again. Amelia starts to cry as well. I feel Dianella leave us, but Jason is right behind me, soothing me. Letting me know he has my back no matter what. I release Amelia from our embrace. I look into her eyes and I see my reflection in hers. We both have our father's eyes, strong and fearless.

"I have something to tell you." I look to Jason. "Is there somewhere we can sit and talk?"

"Absolutely, follow me." He leads us to an office that is three times bigger than my bedroom. It has mahogany finished wood throughout the office. It has a loveseat with two accent chairs surrounding a coffee table. A desk sits in the middle of the room with a bookshelf lining all the walls. They are filled with books and more books. I pull my sister to the loveseat and we sit down.

"Would you like for me to stay or leave?" Jason asks.

"I have to do this on my own. We will come find you once we are done." Jason then walks out and closes the door behind him. I take a deep breath and explain to my sister, my baby sister, what is going on.

"We are working a case where several young girls are disappearing. At first, we couldn't understand the pattern of the deaths or why these girls are being killed. We still don't know why they are being killed, but I found out an alarming connection. They all attended Georgia College at some point, and they all were foster kids from Greenbriar."

"How does this pertain to me?"

"They all look like you, have earrings like yours, go to the same school, very athletic, and were foster kids like you. Does any of this sound familiar?"

"Well, yes, but…"

"No buts; I am placing a detail on you right now."

"What? No, you will not."

"Yes, I will, and I can."

"Lily, no, please… I am never alone. I am always with Dianella either at school or The Grind."

"That brings me to my next question. Why didn't you tell me about Dianella? You always tell me everything."

"Well, you've been busy lately, and to tell you the truth, I need to be able to take care of myself. You have done everything for me. Don't get me wrong, I appreciate everything you have done and will do, but I need to find myself and I don't want to have to keep coming to you for everything. I'm actually planning on moving out of the house. You need your own space. Find someone, go back to school, enjoy your life. You deserve to be happy as well."

"I…I don't know what to say. You are my life. I can't go on if something happened to you."

"I'm not going anywhere. I am staying in Savannah to finish the nursing program. Dianella and I would like to move in together above The Grind at the end of month. She has a large loft with three bedrooms; one is used for the study room where we can practice. I will get a job to help pay rent…"

"Absolutely not. We have enough money to buy the whole city. You will continue to focus on your studies. Let me worry about the cost of living. We are wealthy now; I just don't act like it because I do not want people to treat us differently. Mommy and Daddy left enough for our grandchildren, and I also invested some, so we are well off. Let me talk to Jason. I will work something out with him. I think he said he owns the business and the building with Dianella."

"Okay, I love you, Lily. And I promise to be careful. You taught me very well."

I hold on to her hands in my lap for as long as I can until she pulls away. I know I should be happy, but I feel like shit right now. She is the only reason I want to live and now she is leaving me…well, not really, but it certainly feels like it. She doesn't need me anymore. I have to let her go. She gives me a hug and we both stand up. I hear a knock on the door. Dianella walks in.

"Is everything okay?"

"Yes, everything is okay. I will let you guys go now. Where is your brother?" I ask.

"He is downstairs in the study."

"Okay…and Dianella, you two watch each other's back. There is too much going on and I don't want anything to happen to either one of you."

"Absolutely, my brother filled me in on what's going on. Amelia and I never leave each other's side."

I walk to the door and turn around. I look at both of them. I pray nothing happens or I will shut this city down over my sister. I watch my sister with Dianella. I can see the friendship now. She needs her more than she needs me right now. I'm glad she has someone to reach out to.

I head down the stairs when I notice all the portraits hanging on the wall. Photos of Dianella and Jason and photos of their parents. Jason is the spitting image of his father. My gosh, the resemblance is remarkable. Strong jawline, clean shaven with dark hair, green eyes that makes a rainforest look bland. His father has strong masculine shoulders just like him. I can definitely see where he gets his looks. I head to the living room looking for the study when a hand grabs my wrist and pulls me into a dark room. I slam into a hard body. My breathing picks up because I know exactly who it is. Jason. He runs his finger through my hair and pulls gently, so my neck is produced to him. He drags his lips down my neck, kissing me softly. He pulls me closer to him and I melt into his arms. He holds me with his masculine arms so I won't fall. He presses his lips on mine and invites me to open up. I open and he thrusts his tongue in my mouth, exploring every inch. He tastes of mint and coffee and I want to devour him. We are now breathing incredibly hard when he starts to grab my breasts. They are not extraordinary, just a D cup, but he fondles them like they are the best set of breasts he ever felt. He starts to lift my shirt over my head, and I let him. I don't care that both our sisters are upstairs. I need him to fuck me hard now. He then takes my bra off like a pro. He bends his head between my breasts and licks the valley between them. I start to moan in his ear, running my fingers through his hair. He then flicks my nipple with his tongue and I nearly jump out his arms. He holds me still with his strong arms. My god, that feels so good. He then takes my nipple in between his teeth and sucks and I nearly come all over my panties. I beg him to continue.

"Please don't stop. My god, that feels so good."

"You like that, my love?"

"Yes...god, I love it." He then lifts me up like I weigh nothing and carries me to what I assume is a bed. I never bother asking where we are. I don't care right now. He softly places me on a bed and starts to pull my pants down. He then grabs my panties and pulls those down as well. I am soaking wet with arousal. It's been so long since I've had dick, let alone good dick. He sniffs my arousal and immediately dives between my legs. He is licking and sucking and drinking all of my essence. I am losing my mind. I can't take it anymore. I am about to...

"Yes, come for me. I want to taste you. I've wanted this sweet pussy all night long. Give it to me." Then I explode in his mouth. I reach a high I never reached before. I see stars and feel overwhelming desire. I need more. Just as I come down from my high, he pushes his jeans down over his hips, pulls out a condom, and swiftly slides it on without effort. He fills me with his massive dick. I gasp for air at the entrance. He starts out slow because he knows I am so tight. He then picks up speed; hitting that spot over and over again. Just when I get ready to explode again, he snatches out of me and I feel lost, but not for long. He starts to suck the orgasm out of me, and I fall into bliss. He then enters me again and thrusts and thrusts and thrusts over and over again. I can feel his balls hit the bottom of my ass. I feel my breasts shaking up and down. He leans down and kisses me with all his power while thrusting inside me.

"You are so fucking beautiful. I don't know how I waited this long to have this pussy. You are so tight, and god, you feel good. I can stay here forever, my love."

He continues to thrust into me, and I never want it to end. I've never felt more alive. He is large and thick in size. He fills my walls with pleasure. I've waited so long for someone like him. He is my knight in shining armor, my rock. I need him now and he knows it. He knows that I am broken, and I need something or someone to pick me up. I feel him throbbing inside of me and it is the greatest feeling in the world. I feel tears sliding down my cheeks, not tears of fear, but tears of bliss, tears of the pain I've suffered for the past five years. I feel him come inside of me, the condom separating us, but I still feel how full the condom becomes. He then kisses my tears away, one by one, and in that moment, I feel safe from pain and fear. I feel desired and wanted. I feel alive again. He rolls off of me and goes to the bathroom to clean himself up. I roll to my side and hold on to the covers for dear life. After he is done, Jason comes back to the bed and holds me, cuddles me. I close my eyes without a care in the world.

Chapter 7

Jason

I slip out of bed when I feel the sun grace my face. I let Lily sleep because she needs it. She went through hell last night from thinking she lost her sister to remembering all the memories of when her parents were killed. I knew this was not the time to be a dick to her. She needed me; she needed my strength. I normally never sleep with anyone, but Lily, she is slowly changing me without even knowing it. I am a selfish hard-ass who works, makes money, and fucks. I don't make love, I don't cuddle, I don't fall asleep with anyone in my bed. I just broke all of my rules in one night because she needed me.

I head for the kitchen to start breakfast. Dianella and Amelia left last night and texted me when they made it back to their loft. While I brewed the coffee, I began frying bacon and scrambling eggs. Lily can eat. I've watched her in action. I have no idea how she keeps that firm ass and small waist with thick legs. She must work out, but needless to say, she is one fine butterfly. Just one look from her with those gorgeous eyes and my dick stands at attention. Fuck, I can't get this girl out of my head. She is absolutely no good for me. We work together, for god's sake. I do not need this type of distraction, but she challenges me. She makes me want to be a better man, if not for myself, then for her, her sister, and my sister. All these fucking women in my life are making me soft.

I place the bacon and eggs on a plate with a cup of orange juice and coffee with cream and sugar on a tray, just the way she likes it. I head to my old bedroom. Once I open the door I am presented with the most beautiful vision I've ever seen. She is sitting up in bed with one of my t-shirts. She must have got it out my drawer. She has the longest beautiful brown legs I've ever seen. Her hair is messy from our lovemaking last night and she has this glow that makes the sun seem dull. She smiles at me and I nearly drop the tray and want to fuck right now, but I hold my composure. I place the tray on her lap.

"Oh my gosh, this looks amazing and smells so good. How did you know I love bacon and eggs in the morning?"

"You had breakfast a couple of years ago at The Grind, but you didn't notice me. I was in the back of the restaurant working on the budget at the time. I honestly do not know how you stay in such great shape eating like this every day. But I won't knock it. You look amazing." She blushes around her cheeks. I've just made her feel bashful.

"Thank you. Honestly, I love to dance. I've been a dancer all my life. My favorites are ballet, modern dance, and hip-hop. I combine the three to bring a pleasurable feeling for all. It helps with stress." She picks up the fork and starts to devour her food. The second she takes a sip of her coffee, she falls into what seems like an orgasm. It's the most erotic scene I ever witnessed. I move the tray from her lap, take the coffee cup from her lips, slide my sweats down, place a condom on, get on top of her, and fuck her into the next century. Entering her is like diving into a pool of ecstasy. Her walls are so tight around my dick. I can feel her moisture through the condom. Fuck, she feels so good. I push further into her until I feel my balls hit the bottom of her ass. She's calling out my name…

"Jason, god, Jason."

"Fuck, you feel like heaven." I can feel her tightening up; she is about to come. I love watching her. She makes the most beautiful expressions when I'm pleasing her.

"Come, my love. Come for me, my beautiful butterfly." She then releases and I see the tears streaming down her cheeks. It's the most beautiful thing I've ever seen. I love it when she cries during sex. I know I am making her feel something when she cries. I start to kiss the tears away. Making me harder than I've ever been. I begin to thrust into her over and over again. I can fuck this pussy all day and all night. I want more. I need more. I want to feel her come again.

"Butterfly, I want to feel you come again." I thrust into her harder and on command, she gives me the orgasm of a lifetime. She arches her back and lifts her ass off the bed, pushing me deeper into her. I fall apart and give her what she wants. I come so hard; I feel like I'm about to have a heart attack. Once the rush calms down, I roll off of her and head to the bathroom to clean myself off. At this rate, we will never make it out of this room. I come back into the room and see her naked ass in the air. I walk over, bend down, and thrust my tongue into her wet pussy. She screams out and starts to thrust her pussy into my mouth. She tastes of sweet honey and strawberries. I lick all of her essence. She then starts to come again, and I suck on her clit and make her explode in my mouth. She tastes so good. After her orgasm, she drops on the bed from exhaustion. I climb into bed, wrap my arms around her, and we both drift away.

I awake when I hear my phone ring. I look at the caller ID. It's Detective Knight. I pick up.

"What is it?"

"Rude much?"

"You should be used to my demeanor by now. What do you need?"

"We have a break in the case. We need you in the office."

"Fine, I will be there in twenty." She doesn't know that I am with Lily because her phone starts to ring the second I get off the phone with her. Lily rolls over and reaches for her phone without looking to see who is calling her. Her hair is strewn all over the pillow. God, she looks sexy as hell.

"Hello." There is a long pause. I'm assuming Knight is telling her everything she told me.

"Okay, I am on my way. I will be there...in thirty minutes." She jumps up remembering where she is. "Shit, I need my clothes, toothbrush..." She looks in the mirror. "Shoot, I need a shower."

"Calm down. You and my sister are about the same size. She has clothes upstairs. I have extra toothbrushes in the bathroom. Take a shower in there. I will go get the clothes." She visibly calms down and heads for the bathroom. While the water is running, I go upstairs to get the clothes. I pick out a pair of jeans and a V-neck shirt. This will enhance her attributes. I head back to the bedroom as she walks out the bathroom with nothing but a towel wrapped around her. She is absolutely stunning, hair pulled up in a messy bun. I hand her the clothes. She pulls on the jeans with no panties and I start to lose my mind. I will not be able to function at work today knowing she has nothing under her clothes. She then puts her bra back on and pulls the shirt over her beautiful figure. I can't stop staring, but I know I have to get ready as well. I pull my eyes from staring at her and head for the bathroom.

"I will be in the kitchen waiting for you," she yells.

"Okay, make yourself at home." I step in the shower, running cold water. I need it to calm the fuck down. I feel like a horny teenager who jacks off every waking moment. I need to get my shit together and sooner than later. After lathering my body with my bodywash, I rinse off in the ice-cold water. It definitely does the trick. I turn off the water and step out of the shower. I dry off, put my favorite cologne on, brush my teeth and hair. I throw on my clothes and go downstairs. Lily is standing at the counter cleaning the dishes left in the sink.

"You don't have to do that. We have someone who comes in every day to keep the property looking groomed."

"I don't mind at all. It's the least I can do after you taking care of me yesterday."

"I am always here, Butterfly." I chose that nickname because she reminds me of a butterfly. She is like a flower of the sky, dancing by in a whirl of color. She is born to fly from her nest, to bring beauty so delicate into the warming summer air. As sweet as the nectar she seeks, she raises her wings as an organic clock, each flutter a moment until her time is gone. But she will never leave this earth. She is mine to nurture. She is mine to protect. She is mine.

"Thank you. It's time to go. I am capable of driving now." She grabs the keys out of my hand and walks toward the door, swaying her hips back and forth. She looks sexy in those jeans. I let her lead the way. Her feisty ways are back.

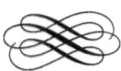

We walk into the office together and Knight looks up like we did something scandalous. I shoot her a deadly look suggesting minding her business.

"Hey, Kim," Lily says.

"Hey, Lily," Kim says with a devilish smile. She whispers in Lily's ear and I can see the blush spreading through her cheeks. She looks so gorgeous when she is embarrassed.

"What did you find with the case?" Lily changes the subject, obviously wanting to ignore her response.

"Our last victim scratched her assailant pretty good and we were able to retrieve DNA. We are now running it through the system to see if we can find a match. It should take a few days.

"Damn it, we don't have a few days. We need this information now!" I yell, pounding my fist on the desk.

"Hold on, let's think for a minute. What can we work with now? We have the scenes; we know what girls he is attracted to and what drives him to continue killing. We have physical evidence as well." Watching Lily get back into action is fascinating. I am an impatient man as she is a well-rounded thinker. She has taken the reins and leading this investigation. Her leadership is astounding. The way she captivates everyone. She isn't even one of us and she already has these guys following her every lead.

"If you didn't notice yesterday, I led to a serious clue that may or may not involve my sister." She passes a picture around so they can see who the person is she is referring to. "She is a beautiful young lady, with long, wavy hair, hazel eyes. She is a student from Georgia College, and she is active with dance and defensive tactics. She does very well in school."

"You basically just described yourself. What makes you think this asshole is not after you?" I ask.

Lily looks at me with peculiar eyes. I can see more green than brown, with a hint of gold flakes. She is in deep thought and trying to find a rebuttal.

"I never finished school. I dropped out for reasons I choose not to share at this moment. I am observant and protective of the people in my life. If this guy wanted me, why not grace me with his presence? Why not come after me, but go after defenseless young women?"

"Like you mentioned earlier, he wants you, but can't have you. Therefore, he is hoping that you will notice him through the girls he offers to you."

Oh, she is pissed now. She is throwing up the walls with a vengeance.

"I would know if someone was after me; furthermore I would destroy this very cowardly person."

"Maybe he knows that, and that is why he is hiding behind these killings. Maybe you are the ultimate prize, not your sister or even the girls he has killed." I see I have crossed the line...

"Because I am merely assisting you on this investigation and not a part of the unit, I will let that assessment fall at the wayside, but know that I will never forget this conversation." And just like that, I lost the battle. "These girls do not deserve such reprehensible deaths. They were on the verge of thriving in their lives; they would have achieved goals, had families, made something of themselves, and for all of that to be taken away because a coward wants to make someone see him is absolutely ridiculous let alone unforgivable."

"He is not looking for forgiveness; he is looking for permission," I say.

"Permission to do what?" asks Knight.

"To be accepted by the one he loves, the one he cherishes the most. That's what he desires, and he will accomplish that goal sooner than later. That will end the killings. That would solve the case. We find his desire, we find him," Lily says eloquently. Sometimes I wonder if she realizes how talented she is. "It's like solving a puzzle, a mystery. He is playing a game and he wants us to solve the mystery.

"I never thought about it like that. I always assumed people do crazy things because of their upbringing or something traumatic happened in their life," Knight says.

"You aren't wrong. People do react differently to trauma in their life or in someone else's life. For example, losing a loved one can set a person in overdrive where they cannot manage their everyday activities, and others move forward without shedding a tear. We all act differently but society expects us to act a certain way. You cannot be a great investigator if you assume everyone acts the same way. What makes you great is thinking outside the box," Lily confesses.

Wow, well said. I would follow her anywhere. I wouldn't admit it to anyone, but I definitely think she should be in this unit, but did I fuck things up because we fucked each other? Will we be able to work together and leave our personal lives outside of work? We shall see.

Chapter 8

Lily

I open my eyes with the sun kissing my face. I love it when the sun rises and falls. It's the most peaceful time of day, and the most colorful time of day. Amelia crosses my mind. I wonder if she is okay, if she has everything she needs. Fuck, I forgot to speak with Jason about her rent. I don't want her to have to want for anything. I will give him a call in a minute. He sometimes pisses me off, but in a way, he is there when I need him. Like last night, I had a total breakdown and he never judged me or made me feel weak. He picked me up and he absolutely blew my mind. I didn't think sex could be so good, so delicious. I can make love to him every night; feel those thick massive hands all over my body, and that thick huge dick is out of this world.

Stop, Lily, get your mind out of the gutter.

I get out of bed and head for the kitchen. I need coffee. I start the Keurig and then call Jason. He picks up on the first ring.

"Hello, Butterfly."

I absolutely love the nickname he has given me. It literally gives me butterflies in my stomach.

"Hi, I need to talk to you about something."

"Shoot."

"Okay, the thing is my sister dropped the bomb on me that she would like to move in with your sister and be roommates. I will pay for all her utilities and rent. I want her focused on school and not trying to pay for her next meal…"

"Stop, Lily. What makes you think I will accept any type of payment from you or your sister? The loft is already paid for. Amelia can stay there as long as she wants."

"We don't do handouts, so I will pay the reasonable amount for rent."

"You can do whatever you want, but I will not accept any money from you. I know how much you get paid, and now you know that I am a very wealthy man."

"Actually, that statement is further from the truth. I know nothing about you, and you know nothing about me."

"Why don't you enlighten me on everything about Lily Matthews."

Why do I always have the compelling need to stick my foot in my mouth around this guy?

"What do you want to know?" I ask.

"What happened the other night?"

Seriously, he would start with that.

"Well...I...I've been struggling with remembering the night of my parents' death. I can remember some things, but not all. It all came flashing back at me, and I became overwhelmed with grief, fear, anger, and any other emotion that a person can feel all at the same time. My sister is my everything, and when I felt the fear of losing her, it almost sent me back to the immense sadness, the unbearable fear and grief that I didn't think I could ever climb out of; the dark, dark hole I fell into only five years ago."

"How do you feel now?"

"Well, honestly you really helped me. You lifted me up, but at the same time you didn't feel sorry for me. You gave me the power to want to find my sister and you helped. Obviously, there are things I didn't know about my sister. I had no idea she was considering my best interest. All along I've been protective of hers. I guess we are protecting each other." It is becoming very easy to talk with him. He makes me feel alive; he makes me feel like I have purpose in life.

"I want to apologize for not being honest with you up front," he says. "I just don't like it when people look at me differently because of my wealth. I choose to be a cop. I love the rush, the adrenaline that it gives me. No, I don't have to work, but I want to."

Wow, I had no idea. Now, he is making me feel like shit. I really need to be honest with him as well.

"Jason, I am wealthy as well. Well, both me and my sister are. After our parents died, they left a significant amount of money and property to us. I don't have to work either, but I chose this work to help myself get out of the crud I was in. I needed to do something meaningful and I felt I could do that by being a cop as well. I dropped out of school because I felt an obligation to protect my sister. To raise her and be there for her. She was sixteen at the time of our parents' death, so I had to fight for custody for her. I did not want her to be raised by strangers. My aunt wanted us to move in with her, but I believe she had an ulterior motive. She wants control of our parents' money. I felt she was always jealous of my mother, her accomplishments, her love for my dad, her experiences."

"So, you can't count on anyone at this point."

"No, I can't. I can only count on myself and my sister."

"Well, you can always count on me. I will and can protect you, Lily." And just like that, I feel myself needing him more than I can ever admit. He complements my strengths and he also complements my weaknesses. I fall into silence because I don't know what to say.

Then I hear the doorbell ring. "Can you hold on just a minute? Someone is at my door."

"Sure, Butterfly."

I go to open the door. I try to hide the fact that I am blushing out of my mind and absolutely bashful at this point. I open the door and there he is, standing at the front step in all his glory. The guy is a god and I want him to be my god. He approaches me, places his phone in his back pocket, grabs me by the waist, and looks intensely into my eyes. Those gorgeous green eyes. He pulls me in and kisses me softly on the lips.

"What am I going to do with you, Butterfly?"

"What do you want to do with me?"

He then picks me up. I wrap my legs around his waist, and he devours me with those incredible lips of his. He pours his deepest secrets in this kiss. He discovers my hidden desires with his tongue. He leans me against the wall and explores my body with his strong, powerful hands.

"Where is your bedroom?"

"Down the hall to the left."

He carries me to my bedroom and gently lays me down. He stands over me and just stares at me. Normally I would feel uncomfortable, but the intensity in his eyes is making me wet in my panties. It's almost like he can see through my wall, through all the bullshit and really see me. He is observing the real me, the vulnerable little shy girl inside. The girl who really wants to scream and release her inner self. I start to drag my hands up and down my body, starting with my legs first then reaching my breasts. I squeeze a little which excites me beyond my wildest dreams. I'm staring into his eyes intensely and find he is enjoying every minute of it. I then glide my fingertips down my stomach, leading to the most intimate part of my body. I spread my lips apart and then start pleasuring myself. My breathing begins to pick up as well as his. He wants to touch me, but this right here is turning him on. He can't take it anymore and grabs my legs, pulls me aggressively, and dives in with his tongue. This is my favorite part. He nips, he tucks, he licks my most inner parts. I arch my back because I want more. I run my fingers through his hair and when he nips at my clit, I pull and scream. I hear him grunt, but that does not stop the assault.

"Come for me, my butterfly. I want to drink all of you." And that one statement takes me over the edge. He is sucking and lapping every part of me. He is devouring my very being. Once the waves start to calm down, he rips open a condom, slides it down his shaft, and opens me wide. He pushes my legs over his shoulder, and he positions himself in the perfect spot. He enters me with such intensity I almost fall apart again.

"Fuck, you feel so good. You taste so good. I can't get enough of you. I want you every waking moment. I need you every single second of the day. You are driving me mad," he says. As he explores my walls, he picks up the speed and rams inside me over and over again.

"Oh my god. Please don't stop." I scream over and over again. He has the perfect rhythm. And just like that, I have the orgasm of a lifetime. Just when I think it can't get better than this, it does.

"Yes, Butterfly. Give it to me. I want to feel you come all over this dick."

I see stars surrounding my eyesight. The colors of the rainbow burst around me like fireworks in the sky. I feel his thickness filling me completely. His dick is so big it hurts, but the pleasure alone is overwhelming. He knows how to work my pussy and I am enjoying every bit of it. I feel my release and I fall into a bliss, a comfort. I never want to leave this feeling. He leans down and gives me the most passionate kiss I ever had. He is not just fucking me; he is making love to me and I am falling hard. I desire more. I want more. I want him. He then releases his seed inside the condom and for a brief moment, I wish he was releasing inside of me. Feeling his seed fill me completely and then feel it run down my legs. He falls on top of me but holds his weight so he doesn't crush me. He stays inside of me like he never wants to leave this place. It's become home for the both of us. He then reluctantly rolls off of me and heads to my bathroom. He cleans himself off and then returns to my bed. He wraps his arms around me and then cuddles me close to his chest. He sweeps my hair from my forehead and admires my features. He runs the tips of his fingers down my face and places a soft kiss on my forehead.

"You are so beautiful, Lily."

"Thank you. You're not so bad yourself." He chuckles as I downplay his sexiness. He knows he is gorgeous, and his arrogance is only a game to me. I find it fascinating. "Tell me something about yourself," I say. He physically tenses up, but he responds to the statement.

"Dianella and I are basically in the same boat you are in. We lost our mom as well. Our dad left my mom and us when we were very young. We were adopted by Allison Taylor, and she and my sister saved me. I was pretty much headed down a spiraling path with no care in the world. Once our adoptive mother passed away, I've taken care of Dianella most of her teenage life. I never got close to anyone. Always pushed anyone away when it became too intimate. I didn't want random people in Dianella's life. I wanted her to achieve every goal that was set by her and our moms. She is more handsy than I am. I'm straight up with you. I will never sugar-coat anything. You get all or nothing from me. I've made my wealth through my best friend, Ryan. He took the money our moms left us and turned it into what we have now. You are looking at a multimillionaire who still wants to kick ass, who wants to solve cases, who wants the day-to-day bustle of the street life." Fascinated, I lie back and listen. Every once in a while, he places a kiss to the back of my head. "I was up for promotion several times, but I always turned it down."

"Why did you turn them down? That's a great opportunity."

"Like I said, I love the bustle every day. I don't want to sit behind a desk, going to meeting after meeting. I want to be in the grunt of it."

Wow, I never realized how alike we are. We are both wealthy people but want to get our hands dirty. Who would have thought? Jason looks around my room and notices my back porch, my sanctuary. He gets up and walks over to the door, totally naked. He is like a walking god. Not only is he handsome from the depth of his green eyes, but he can be gentle with the softness of his voice. He is handsome from his generous opinions to the touch of his hand upon my own. I love the way his voice quickens when he sparks with new ideas or when he is enjoying one of mine. There are times when he seems to lose himself for a moment and quite forget the mask he wears for others. What he is, what is beautiful about him, comes from deep within; it makes me want to feel how his lips move in a kiss, how his hands follow the curves of my body. He has the kind of face that will stop you in your tracks. I guess he must get used to that, the sudden pause in a person's natural expression when they look his way followed by overcompensating with a nonchalant gaze and a weak smile.

Breaking my train of thought, he says, "Let's go outside and sit on the porch."

Is he crazy? We are totally naked. "Let me put something on first. I will meet..." He grabs my hand and yanks me into his solid body. I grunt at the intrusion and he gives me that little smirk he does when he is being cunning.

"You don't need anything; I will keep you warm if that's what you are worried about."

"I have neighbors, you know. We are not isolated in the wilderness."

"Actually, your closest neighbor is a half mile down the road. You have the most breathtaking view out your window, and you can't pass this opportunity up."

Hesitantly, I open the door and step out. The weather is warm with a breeze that takes my hair on a journey. I turn around and the wind blows my hair across my face. Jason grabs me by the waist and leans in and places the most passionate kiss on my lips. So soft and full. He knows how to kiss a girl. He pulls away and guides me to my loveseat overlooking the marsh lands and palm trees.

"How do you do it?" he asks.

"How do I do what?"

"How are you able to step in the shoes of victims or suspects and give a complete analysis of their behavior, their life, their likes and dislikes?"

No one has ever asked me that because I never really showed someone my methodical nature. "I look at things differently than the average person. I am very observant, and I never leave a stone unturned. I look at the bigger picture. I look within the mind of the victim and the suspect. I want to know why."

"You have this intense alertness to all elements of the environment around you. This will lead you to incisive insights and shrewd decisions."

"Thank you...I guess." It almost sounded like a punch in the stomach than an actual compliment.

"No, no, no... I didn't mean what you think. I am fascinated by you. You are careful about details. You want to know the specifics about a situation before you are willing to make a decision. This will help you and hurt you in a way."

"How?"

"Well, there are cases that need to be solved very quickly and then there are cases that you can take your time. In this instance, we need to solve this case now before anyone else gets hurt," he says.

I sit up and just stare at him.

"You don't think I know that? These girls are a spitting image of my sister. I want this guy dead or put away. And to be honest, you wouldn't be this far without me." I stand up, prepared to walk away, and he grabs my hand, turning me around. I fall into his lap and he crushes his lips on mine, devouring my mouth like he didn't just fuck me thirty minutes ago. I visibly fall apart, and I forget the reason I was even angry. I straddle my legs around his waist and pour everything I am into this kiss. I give him the promise of realness, of the primal desire that lives in us all. And with it I tell him that I am awake, connected within. This kiss is not innocent; it's fiery, passionate, and demanding. I want to pull away before I lose myself, but I can't seem to. In this obsessing moment, my senses have been seduced and I can no longer think straight.

"Lily," he whispers slowly, prolonging each letter as if to savor it. I smile, my heart fluttering at his voice as I clasp my hands on either side of his face. Never before has my name ever felt so wonderful, I think, as I lean in for another. I want more. I desire more.

He picks me up with those powerful arms and places me on the loveseat. He walks away and I feel abandoned. I need him near me. He comes back a second later with a condom on his pretty dick. Shit, I was so far gone I was ready to fuck him without protection, again. I wonder what it would feel like if we had. To feel it expand in my inner walls, throbbing with excitement. I look up and I am blessed with the grace of such a beautiful dick, larger than my body can tolerate, but meaningful enough to never want to fuck another person again.

"Get on your knees," he demands, and like a dutiful submissive, I oblige my sex god. I get on my knees on the loveseat and perk my ass up in the air like a roast served on a platter. I then look over my shoulder and look into those beautiful green eyes. And like a simple schoolgirl slut, I drip my essence down my leg.

"Shit, you are sexy as fuck. I can't wait no longer; I need to be in that sweet, wet pussy now." He glides through my slickness with no problem at all. Entering me with force I didn't think was possible. I instantly buck forward and he grabs my hips to keep me still. He then thrusts again and stop to savior the incredible feeling we share together. He continues to take me to my limit and then stop. He is absolutely driving me insane and pleasuring me all at the same time. He is teasing me, but this must be torture for him as well. But you got the right one, I will not give in. He will not break me.

"Aw, you feel so good. I can be buried in this pussy all day and not give a rat's ass about anyone or anything else. I am going to take you nice and slow."

"If you go any slower, I'm going to slip into a coma," I say with impatience. I get a chuckle out of him for that one. He does this smirk that shows his dimples. That smirk is his most alluring feature. I call it the panty-dropper smirk. I wouldn't dare tell him. He begins to pick up the pace and takes me to a high I thought I could not go before. My head falls back. Thrust after thrust and at that very moment I reach my climax, I feel a tear run down my face. Damn it, these tears are so annoying. I cannot be normal like everyone else. I have never been a crier during sex, but this guy just brings it out of me. I begin to shake uncontrollably and squeeze the pretty dick inside of me. I arch my back and when I think I am over, he pulls out and goes down on me, eating my pussy like the very first time.

"Give it to me, Butterfly. Stop holding back. Give me all of you." And at that very moment, I collapse on the loveseat because I cannot take it anymore.

"I'm not done yet, my butterfly." He flips me over and hovers over me, staring me in my eyes. The stare is so intense, I want to look away, but then again, I can't. He hypnotizes me with the color of the sweet jungle in his eyes and as he takes all of me, he thrusts his large thick dick inside of me again and again and again. I scream out and for a moment I forget we are on the back porch. I find that I actually don't care anymore. I don't care who hears us or sees us. I want this man, and no one will take him from me. He is mine.

Chapter 9

Jason

Abright and early drive to the office is always soothing and peaceful for me. I am able to think more clearly through my head of bullshit. But I find myself not able to clear my head of Lily, my butterfly. She has consumed my every thought, my every being. I find myself wanting to be near her, protect her from her deepest fears. Never have I ever thought about another woman past the first round of fucking, let alone remembering their name. Lily is something different. She has captured my soul and stolen it without me even knowing. I find myself wanting to know everything about her, like what's her favorite color and shit like that. Why the fuck should I even care about what color she likes. I am turning into a pussy because of this woman and I don't know how that even happened.

I pull into the parking lot and see the one and only S500 in the parking lot. What do you know, Lily has really stepped up to becoming a sharp investigator. Not only is she talented with profiling suspects, but she is talented with profiling our victims as well. She can reach within their inner soul, mind, and body to find their deepest secrets, wants, desires. I find that fascinating even though she doesn't realize her incredible talent.

I walk into the building and find Lily staring at the victimology board. She is in extremely deep thought. I don't even think she realizes that I am here. I would hate to scare the hell out of her, but my inner demon is willing to catch her when she does jump. I stand there just watching her every move, her every expression, her every thought process. She then moves to the white erase board and starts writing her thoughts on the board. She has a habit of talking out loud and recording herself and when she makes a discovery, she writes her point down on the board.

"The earrings represent something, but what? He has a person in mind, a lover, a mother, someone he wishes was his lover. And the blanket wrapped like a pillow. Why cashmere? Does the expensive quality of the blanket mean something?"

She continues to brainstorm. "He is trying to protect their image. He doesn't want the girls' image to be destroyed. The girls are fully dressed and not provocatively. The girls are placed in areas where they can be found, but how does no one see this suspect place the bodies?"

"Because they are oblivious of their surroundings. They only see what they want to see," I announce. Lily turns around and almost jumps out of her skin. The look on her face is so alluring. I want to fuck her right here on the desk.

"Jesus, you scared the hell out of me."

"Oblivious of your surroundings," I say with sarcasm. Rolling her eyes, she just turns around and goes back to her routine.

"I am here early waiting on the forensics report. Why are you here?" she asks.

"Same reason." Lie on my part. I knew she would be here, and I wanted to be in her presence. Smell her hypnotizing perfume.

"Well, it should be here in a few minutes. I am desperate to find out the DNA under our last victim's nails. This is our big break all because she fought back. She fought for her life and in turn we shall give her justice. We shall give her peace." She is very passionate about this case, but I am afraid she may be too close to the case. I need to keep an eye on her. Protect her from herself.

"I also believe the placement of the bodies is significant. Each body is placed either near a bed of lilies or placed inside the bed of lilies. I find that interesting because of the name of the flower. Do you think he is trying to send me a message?"

"Oh, no you don't," I say. "You nearly chopped my head off for merely suggesting this same thing. However, you have a point. I was thinking the same thing. What about the note you found? Pull that out of evidence. It should have been scanned. Let's dissect it together. We do not know what the motive is just yet, but hopefully this note and the DNA will come back with some answers."

Lily pulls up the note and sends it to the big screen.

"Tonight, the city is ours, it's true

A dreamland created for just me and you
There will be something sweet as pie
Where you find something good to eat for you and I
As we savor our time much long overdue."

"What does this mean?" Lily goes into deep thought trying to process the note. "This sounds like a date. Maybe a first date at a restaurant or café? *Tonight, the city is ours...* This is a romantic evening with someone you love or want to be with. *A dreamland created for just me and you...* This feels like a fantasy. It can't possibly be reality or true in the writer's mind. *There will be something sweet as pie, where you find something good to eat for you and I...* This reminds me of a bakery or café, somewhere where people hang out to get delicious treats. This sounds like your café, The Grind," she announces.

"Wait a minute, so you are telling me that this crazy asshole is using my business for his sick games?" I say with disbelief in every word. What the fuck is going on? This is fucking crazy and we are crazy for even thinking it.

Lily ignores me. "*As we savor our time much long overdue.* He thinks they belong together and the only way they will be together is if he gets her attention. These girls are not messages, they are gifts to his true love. He is helping her see him in a knight-in-shining-armor type of way. Come on, we need to go to the café."

"Wait, just a minute." I stand in front of her, blocking the passage to the door. "Let's think about this first. What are we saying here? Are we saying that this sick dude is after one of us?"

"No, I am not saying that, but we have something to do with this case and if we do not figure it out, there will be more deaths of young girls. So, Jason, please come with me. I need your help. These girls need your help." She pleads with me. In that moment I can see the need for my help, my strength to get her through this investigation. I don't understand it, but I will do anything to help her, protect her.

"Okay, let's go. I will call Knight and have her meet us there. We need all the help we can get."

Chapter 10

Lily

We arrive at The Grind, when it finally hits me. My life is twisted and fucked up. Not only did I lose both my parents, drop out of college, raise a teenage girl by myself, and spend most days putting bad guys away, I also have never really been in love. Like, really in love. I find that I shy away or push it away the second it gets too hard or too tough. I had love in my life. My family loved me and that is all I need; that's all I ever needed. But now I am finding friendship in Kim and Jason. It's weird how they squeezed themselves through my walls and entered my life with a breath of fresh air. Kim is like a sister; I can tell her things and she can tell me things and we can hold each other's secrets. Jason, on the other hand, is something different. He makes me want to be better, to do better, to strive for more. He has opened me up to so many possibilities and I am enjoying it.

While we walk up to the front door, Kim pulls up.

"Hey, Kim."

"Hey, Lily, what's up?"

"Well, I reread the note that I found at the last scene. It had clues in it that sent us here to find. I'm not sure what that is at this moment, but I think I will know what it is when I find it. Make sense?"

"Yeah, that makes sense. I will follow your lead and record everything you say. It actually helps when we go back to the office."

"Yes, I find that recording myself helps me remember things, little things that I might have missed any other time. It helps me keep things in order." We both walk in after Jason.

The welcome scent of coffee wafts through the air, calling to my weary legs to come take a rest. A metallic table reflects the sun, almost blinding me for a second. As I take a seat, I am surrounded by mountains of plastic and paper bags which hold the contents of guilt-ridden people's shopping. They are taking a break from spending money they don't have. The sun heats the chairs and it feels comforting and warm. I look around and see a waitress who is beautiful and young. Must be a college student. She lights up when she sees Jason. I see that spark in her eyes and she runs to hug him like she wants to jump his bones. He kindly pushes her away and, in that moment, I need more than caffeine; whiskey is now consuming my mind and I am furious. I don't even understand why, but I have a need to claim my property, my man. She teeters all over him in a miniskirt and a top that leaves nothing to the imagination. Her heels are so impractical for someone who will be on their feet all day.

But she knows they make her legs look amazing. I take solace in the fact that her feet will be aching later. Her face is fixed into a false smile. She has too much makeup on and I doubt she can even remember the natural color of her hair. I walk up to Jason's side and clear my throat. Making it obvious that I am pissed to him but plaster a smile on my face for her.

"Hi, my name is Lily. How are you?" I shake her hand and she just bounces up and down, allowing her perky little breasts to bounce with her every movement.

"Hi, I'm Maggie." She stands there awkwardly, so I start to talk.

"Can I steal this handsome guy from you just a moment? I have a question for him."

"Oh, yes of course. Do y'all need anything? I can bring it right out."

"That would be great, Maggie. Get us some scones and coffee, mine black and theirs with cream and sugar," he tells her.

"Coming right up, boss." She then turns and bounces right off.

I look up at Jason and laugh.

"Shut up."

"What?"

"You know what. The girl has a crush on me."

"I think she has a little more than a crush on you. She wants to jump your bones."

Ignoring me, he changes the subject. "Okay, we are here. What are we looking for?"

I let the interrogation go and dive into what I do best. I start to look around. The noise from traffic invades my thoughts. Carriers making deliveries, clattering and banging as the drivers empty their cargo without a care. The heavy smell of coffee fills my nostrils and I long to inhale my own sweet aroma of coffee. More people carrying bags, spending more money. Arguing with their partners loudly as the stress gets to the most patient of people. The café in comparison seems calm. It's a place where people want to come and relax. They want to leave the bustle of their surroundings and enjoy the most delicious cup of coffee in the world. I wonder how Jason does it. Nevertheless, I look around and find a piece of paper sticking out from behind a picture frame of Jason and his sister. I get up and walk over to the picture frame and pull the piece of paper out. It is folded just like the other one. I open it up and read the content:

"It's time now to feel the burning of the heat
Your search is yet still impossibly incomplete
Go claim a prize that desires all mine
Where temperatures rise where I lie
To continue this fumy retreat."

I turn to Jason and Kim and I immediately know this is bad.

"It's another clue."

"What the fuck is this guy doing? I don't play fucking games with no one," Jason says with frustration in his tone.

"Calm down, we have to play this game to stop another girl from being killed," I say.

"I agree," Kim says.

"Okay, I will calm down, but I do not like where this is going. I will not put any of you in danger…"

"It's kind of our job to be in danger, remember? We are all cops, so stop trying to protect us and let's work on this together." Jason is pissing me off, thinking I can't do my job. I'm a cop just like him. I can and will protect myself and probably his ass as well.

"Now that we are done with that, we need to figure this riddle out. I really believe this has something to do with the murders." I look at the note again. *It's time now to feel the burning of the heat, your search is yet still impossibly incomplete…* "I think this has to do with the other scenes. We are missing something. But, what? *Go claim a prize that desires all mine where temperatures rise where I lie to continue this fumy retreat.*"

"I think we should head to the other scenes to see if we are missing anything. That way we can say we have covered all our bases," Kim says.

"I agree. We are missing something, and I will not be able to sleep until I find what that might be."

"Okay, let's go. I will drive," Jason says. We head out of the café and I run directly into my old partner, Officer Anthony Page. Page is one of those men who exudes sexuality, intentionally or not, and used to send me into overdrive at times. I find that now that I have had a taste of Jason, I don't really find Page attractive anymore. Now, don't get me wrong, he is that eye candy a woman craves, but he is not my eye candy anymore. All I see is another good-looking black man standing six feet two with coffee brown eyes, jet black hair, a strong jawline, and a Romanesque nose. He always kept to himself but opened up a little with me once he got to know me. People thought he was a little weird at times when we rode calls together, but quiet most of the time.

"Oh, I'm sorry for bumping into you. I didn't see you. How is it going?" I ask. This feels so awkward with Jason and Kim standing here watching this awful transaction.

"Hey, Matthews. I'm good, just came by to see how you were doing in your new position."

"Not quite my new position, but I am working towards that. You know I always wanted to be in investigations."

"Yes, I remember. Sarge got me riding with Hicks. He really doesn't get me like you did." He looks pitiful right now. Like he lost his best friend. Am I his only friend?

"How did you know we would be here?" I ask. "I don't remember telling you I would be."

"This is your favorite spot. I took a chance in running into you. I'm glad I did." Right, this is my favorite spot.

"We are heading out right now. Working on a case. But we can go have drinks later if you want?"

"You may not have time for that, Matthews. The captain is pressing us to get this case solved," says Jason. He is staring at Page with this clenched jaw. It's almost like he is jealous of him. Could he be jealous? No, he can't. We are just casually fucking.

"Oh, yes, he is right. We are pretty busy. I can call when I am free. Is that good with you?" Why do I feel like I just let the most important person in my life down, not that he is that person to me? I just get a weird vibe from Page and Jason.

"Absolutely, I can wait." He stares in my eyes for a second and then turns and walks away with his shoulders slumped down like a wounded dog.

"That was really weird," Kim says.

"Yeah, once you get to know him, he is really a nice guy. He never opened up to me before, but I get this feeling that something happened to him in his past. He doesn't really trust people. I've been so consumed with this case, I neglected to call him."

"You shouldn't have to feel obligated to keep in touch with your partners. You will have many as you progress on this department," Jason says.

"I disagree with you, but I do understand that I will make many more connections on this department as I grow," I reply.

We all get in the car and drive to the first scene, Madison Square. Madison Square has always been my favorite square to sit and watch weddings, listen to the birds chirp, and watch people of all walks of life taking pictures and exploring the history of

Savannah. It's a small roundabout with beautiful exotic plants strategically placed in the square to give it a feel of a rain forest. As I look closer, I see lily-like plants all around the square. There is a plethora of history, and even some rumored hauntings, in and around the square as well as a great selection of restaurants and shops. There is a coffee shop at the southeast corner called Gryphon; across from there is Shop SCAD. SCAD has pretty much taken over the city, buying up all the property. But in a way, they have given Savannah character as well as keeping the historical vibe of our quant little city.

Breaking my train of thought, Kim distracts me with mundane questions. "What was that back there? It seems like your ex-partner has a thing for you."

"No, I don't think so. He's just misunderstood. Sometimes people find him different because he keeps to himself, but he is a really good person."

"How well do you know him?"

"Well, we have been partners for only three months because his last partner filed a complaint against him. Something about stalking, but I never really got into rumors. He doesn't bother me. We usually keep to ourselves and back each other up on calls. Every once in a while, we would go have a drink or a coffee. But that's it." I continue to look around for clues to the case or these mysterious notes.

"Well, be careful. I get a bad vibe from him."

"Okay, I will be careful. Why is everyone concerned about my welfare, like I'm some fragile glass. I can very much take care of myself and have been doing so for many years now."

"Don't mean to piss you off, just looking after a friend."

Oh gosh, I did it again. All she is doing is looking after me, and here I am being a bitch.

I stop what I am doing and look up at her. "I'm sorry. I'm just under a lot of stress with my sister leaving the house, me getting my memory back, and dealing with all these deaths. I didn't mean to snap on you."

"It's okay, really. I completely understand."

"Let's start looking around to see if we missed anything," I suggest. Jason was still sitting in the car talking on the phone with someone. It looked very important. Kim and I split up and start searching the grounds, plant beds, and trash cans. I start with the lily-like plants. I have a feeling the killer wanted me to come back and search these areas. I leaf through the plants and at first, I am going to give up; the minutes pass by and I find nothing, but then something catches my eye.

"Kim," I call out. "Look, I found another piece of paper folded right here in the plants."

She grabs her camera from around her neck and starts taking pics of the scene. We treat everything like a crime scene just in case we come across something that is important whether it's small or big. I put my gloves on, open the piece of paper, and read the passage:

"Let's set the mood for desire
A dreamy, relaxing prelude
Something delectable and nice
Where bubbles and oils entice
And passion and strength are renewed."

"This sounds like a fountain or a jacuzzi or a whirlpool. Kim, where was the second body found?"

"It was found in Columbia Square," Kim says.

Columbia Square… It is hard to imagine that this small square is in the middle of the bustling downtown streets with its ambient atmosphere and serene fountain, nestled within the northeast quadrant of the Historic District. It's a perfect place to hide a body or place a body without anyone noticing.

"Let's keep looking. We may find something else. Then we need to head to Columbia Square." We continue searching the grounds and then the trash cans but come up empty. I have a feeling because we waited so long to come here and brushed these early murders off, we missed valuable clues. I normally would be pissed off, but I don't have time to argue. Both Kim and I get in the car while Jason is still on the phone, talking to someone in reference to one of his cases. I tune him out and drive to Columbia Square just a couple of blocks from the office. Jason finally gets off the phone and we brief him on what we found.

"So, those cases were connected. Fuck, this is just fucking great. I told that fuck wad that there was something familiar with these murders, but he wouldn't believe me. He told me to leave the cases alone."

"Who told you that?" Both Kim and I are now confused as hell.

"Captain Hill. He wanted me to focus my attention on cases that mattered. His words, not mine."

"What an asshole. We probably could have stopped this long ago if we just treated every murder the same."

"I agree, but he is the captain. Can't really tell him to fuck off, but we must dot our I's and cross our T's before we bring this to him."

I pull up next to Columbia Square and get out of the car, anxious about finding the next clue. I live for this stuff. The adrenaline alone gives me a high I crave every single day. I know people think I'm crazy and insane, but there is only one type of person who would run toward danger, and I am that type of person. I always have been.

Jason walks up behind me and whispers, "I need you right fucking now. Come to my house after we leave here." I suddenly shiver with all the butterflies running in my stomach. My hairs stand on my arms and I instantly get wet from the mere demand of his voice.

"Stop, you are making me lose focus. We have work to do." Brushing him off even though I want to fuck him right here right now as well.

"I'm not stopping until you agree to come over." He blows behind my ear and I nearly jump out of my skin.

"Okay, okay. I will stop by. Now please, let me concentrate." With a smug grin on his face, Jason backs up with his hands raised like he is surrendering to my commands and starts to walk away. He is such a smartass.

We all start to search around the fountain. I know the next clue is somewhere near the fountain. And there it is sticking out of one of the bricks. A normal person would have walked right past it, but because I am not normal, I find it immediately, a piece of paper folded and shoved between the bricks in the fountain.

"I found it."

"Perfect, I will take the pictures."

Jason puts his gloves on and prepares to grab the piece of paper. I get to the clue first.

"Too slow, Detective Hall. In this job you have to be quicker than that." Giving him my best smile playfully, I open the piece of paper. And it reads:

"Cancel your plans, my darling
And set time apart from before
I'll even give you a little head start
Think fast, I am quick.
Fat, I am slow, and wind is my foe.
You're almost at the very end, my darling,
But this is where your guest must deploy."

Our phones ping with a message.

Chapter 11

Jason

“The DNA test is here.” Lily scans over the email. “We need to head back to the office and then figure out this other clue. Kim, bag the evidence.”

“Yes, ma’am,” says Knight.

I’ve watched how Knight responds to Lily and how they interact with each other. They really work very well together. Knight is a promising detective, but Lily shows leadership and desire. She craves this job; she needs this job like a lifeline. I am afraid she may need it too much. What will happen when she finally solves this case? Will she let that desire overwhelm her. Will she focus on something else? I do not want to lose her on this team, but what if it hurts her more than it helps her? I want to protect her with all my being. I will protect her no matter what, but can I protect her from herself? Hell, what am I saying? We are just fucking, or are we? My dick stands at attention every time I am around her, thinking about her, touching her, watching her. Fuck, I am obsessed with a piece of ass. I never in my life cared, let alone remembered a chick's name after a round or two in the sheets. Now I can't even keep my dick in my pants for one moment with this girl. Not just any girl, the girl. She is my butterfly, my olive branch, my whole being. Get your head out of the gutter. We have work to do. We can come out and play later. I grab the keys from Lily.

"I'm driving."

She shoots me a death look but doesn't say anything.

Knight gathers the evidence and then places it in the trunk of the car. Once she gets in, we all head back to the office. Lily damn near jumps out the car before I can put it in park.

"Whoa, slow down. The email isn't going anywhere."

"The quicker we read that email, the quicker we can find this killer."

"I know but we have to slow down before we hurt ourselves or overlook something. I'm not trying to stop you, Lily," I say. "I'm trying to guide you with direction. Slow is fast, fast is slow and sloppy. Got it?"

Rolling her eyes, like she wants to punch me in the throat, she answers, "Got it."

I finally put the car in park and then we all exit the vehicle, anxious to find out what's on the email. We enter the building, and Lily uses her access card to let us in the office. We head straight for the computer. Knight already has her computer up, so we gather around her. The email reads:

Detective Hall,

Certain non-typical sources of DNA, or what we call forensic samples, can be more difficult to extract from than others, such as sperm from sheet, fingernails, toothbrushes, etc. However, once the human DNA has been isolated and extracted from its source, whether using a forensic sample or a simple oral swab, the DNA test will provide the exact same level of accuracy. In other words, the accuracy of the result does not depend on the type of DNA sample used. Below you will find the results.

Unknown suspect's DNA is 99% accurate to Anthony Page.

DNA was found in the nail bed of the victim and cross-referenced with positive hits through GCIC/NCIC employee records, criminal records, and custodial records.

If you have any questions, please let us know.

Officer Jane Day

I immediately look in the direction of Lily. She intensely becomes rigid and stiff. Her skin is ghostly pale. Her breathing is labored and quick. Tears well up in her eyes. I call out to her. "Lily… Lily?" She doesn't move; she is stuck in a dimension and cannot release herself. I grab her by the shoulders and try to have her focus on me, but then she grabs my arm and flips me on the floor like I was trying to hurt her. My body slams on the floor so hard, I think I might have broken something. I get back on my feet and grab her again. This time with force. Shaking her to snap out of it. She finally brings life into her beautiful hazel eyes and focuses on me and finally realizes who I am. She wraps her arms around my waist and holds on for dear life. I know in that moment, she needs me. I am her lifeline and I will never let her go or leave my eyesight. I have to admit, she is one strong woman. She surprised the hell out me and I will never underestimate her strength again.

"Knight, get Lily a chair and a bottle of water. Get me Captain Hill on the phone as soon as possible."

"Yes, sir. How is this even possible? He did not come up on our radar for known persons in these victims' lives. Lily and I literally just talked about him. I felt some weird vibes from him earlier today," Kim admits.

"I know, but my concern right now is Lily. Send a car to Amelia and Dianella's loft. Tell them I need them to head home right now. I will explain later why. I'm taking Lily to my house for now. Knight, grab what you can and bring everything to my house. I do not know who we can trust at this point."

"I'm fine." Lily tries to stand up on her own. "This cannot be. He is my partner, for god's sake. How can he be killing all these people, all these girls, right under my nose and I don't even know about it? There is something else we are missing."

Lily is right, we are missing something, but I also always got a bad feeling about that guy. He is always too concerned about her. Showing up at random times, watching her intensely.

"Here, take this bottle of water and sit down. I don't need you passing out on me."

She takes the bottle of water and downs it in seconds. "Happy?" she says sarcastically.

"Yes, I am. Now, we are leaving." I don't give her any room to argue. We both get into my car and we head to my loft. It is more secure than her house. While driving to the house, my phone rings. It's Captain Hill.

"Hey, Captain. I need to run something by you before we get too involved in this case. We received the DNA results. It came back to Officer Anthony Page, Matthews' old partner. Knight is currently cross-checking the findings, running it through our database. I'm taking Matthews to my loft right now. I don't want to take any chances."

"Thank you for letting me know. Keep Matthews with you and don't let her leave your sight. If this cop is affiliated with murders, then I don't want her getting herself killed."

"Of course. I will not let her out of my sight."

"And Detective Hall?"

"Yes, sir?"

"Great work. This is what we are looking for in a sergeant."

"Thanks, sir, but I won't be taking the sergeant's exam. I like where I am now."

"Okay, but if you ever change your mind, the job is yours."

"I appreciate it." I hang up the phone with the captain and then look at Lily. I can tell she has so much on her mind. She is literally going through every time she was with this guy, trying to find clues or anything she might have missed. So, I decide to interrupt her internal terror.

"Lily, what are you thinking about?"

"Well, I'm trying to figure out when my partner have the time to kidnap a young lady or lure a young lady to him. He convinces her to take pictures in wedding dresses, and then kills her. He then takes the body to a very well-known, open area where he wants me to find it so he can have me. Does that really make sense?" she asks more to herself than to me. "He had me every day of the week for hours. He could have just asked; he could have said he was interested. Why go to these lengths to make me notice him? I noticed him, for god's sake. He was my fuck-ing partner. Hell, he *is* my fucking partner. Why kill innocent women to prove to me that he wants me? Now I want nothing to do with him. Why would he think I would want this? Fuck, this is so fucked up."

I just let her vent because I know this is what she needs. She needs to talk it out to make sense of all this. I have to agree with her on a lot of it. This is fucked up and she is right, why can't Page just come to her. He damn well better not come to her now. She is mine and I will do anything to protect her.

"Lily, has it occurred to you that you are a little intimidating and that it might not be that easy to approach you?"

"Wha—"

"Wait, I know what you are about to say. I'm not saying you are impossible, but maybe he didn't know how to approach you. Maybe this is the only way in his mind to get your attention.

Maybe he feels that you will respect him more if he goes to the lengths he is going to come after you. You said you've been partners for three months, right?"

"Yes, but—"

"And that you thought he was a little stand-offish, but became a good friend after getting to know him, right?"

"Yes."

"Did his behavior change in any way that might not be so alarming before, but could be a clue now?"

"Well, I talked a lot about wanting to become a detective. I told him I felt that I was being passed over because of my past. He seemed to genuinely care and wanted me to achieve my goal. He was more so my biggest fan besides my sister."

"Is that all you can remember about what he was like, if he was going through anything?"

"Actually, yes. He said he was having issues with a relative. He didn't say who, but he said he was taking care of it. I asked him if he needed my help with anything, and he said no. I asked about his family and he always shied away. Like he was ashamed or grew up in a bad situation. I know how life can be sometimes, so I never pressed him on the subject. He was always interested in my life or my family's life. I never really opened up to him like that because I...I guess I was ashamed as well."

"Why do you feel ashamed?"

"Because I could never remember what really happened to my mom and dad. I thought people would think I was weak or broken or couldn't be trusted to be partners because I would forget crucial information on a case. That is why I always record myself. I don't want to forget anything... Wait, I recorded our conversations! Not to be creepy, but because I didn't want to forget. He said it was okay if I did. Let's stop by my house. I have the thumb drives there."

I hesitate at first because I don't want to put Lily in any danger, but she is right. We need those thumb drives if we are going to figure this out. I do a U-turn and head for President Street east toward her house on the island.

Lily sits back and watches the trees pass by through the passenger window. I take her hand and place it on my lap and rub it to give her comfort. I know this is overwhelming for her and I do not want to make things worse. If this is all I can do to comfort her, I will. She then starts to rub my leg further and further up my thigh. I touch her hand and she looks at me with those beautiful hazel eyes. I love the gold flakes in her eyes with a hint of green.

"Are you sure you want to do this? We don't—"

"I'm absolutely sure. I need to feel you. I want to feel you." She begins to undo my belt and zip my pants down. I try my best to focus on the road. I want to give her what she wants, but I don't want to get us killed in the process. She continues her assault on my pants. Once she frees my dick, I instantly get hard as a rod. She wraps her petite hand around my shaft and then starts working it up and down. She takes off her seat belt and leans over. She flicks her tongue over my tip. I nearly swerve off the road.

"Concentrate, Jason, I want you to enjoy this, but I also need you to pay attention to the road."

"That's easier said than done."

"I have faith in you." She peeks up through her eyelashes and I damn near fall apart.

"Okay, I will concentrate."

"Good." She flicks my dick again and I manage to control myself. She then takes her tongue down my shaft and places her lips around my dick. And then she begins to suck and lick and suck and lick. I try my best to not come all over her mouth and then she says the magic words.

"I want to taste your come on my tongue. I want to drink your power, taste your essence, feel you throb in my mouth." And just like that I fucking come so hard in that pretty little mouth of hers. My dick throbbing at the very warmth of her incredible mouth. She drinks all of me and starts sucking life back into my dick. She is nipping and tucking at me like I do to her and now I understand why she completely loses her mind. This feels so fucking great. I need to get us to the house right now. I want to fuck that sweet pussy of hers, but first I'm going to do what she's doing to me, teasing the hell out of me.

I pull up in the driveway, lift her up, and take her mouth inside mine. I kiss her hard and explore every inch of her being in this one kiss. I break loose abruptly.

"Get out and go straight to your room. I want you butt ass naked by the time I get there." She does as I say and scoots right out the car and heads for her bedroom, leaving the door open for me. I pull up my pants and zip them up. As I head to the house, I see something at the corner of my eye. I look over to the bushes and see something move. I draw my duty weapon and point it at a low ready. As I approach the bushes, a squirrel jumps out and runs up a tree. I nearly jump out of my skin and am damn glad I didn't pull the trigger. Close call. I re-holster my weapon and head for the front door. I need to calm down and the only thing that will calm me down right now is a good fuck from my pretty little butterfly.

Chapter 12

Lily

Jason stalks into my room, stripping his clothes off one by one. I did exactly what he asked of me. I am butt ass naked with my ass pointing to the ceiling, downward dog position. Those yoga positions have come in handy. I look over my shoulder and look deep into his eyes, chips of emerald ice: sharp, cold, heated. His desire is overwhelming with lust and it makes my body reacts to the heat penetrating from his body. He hovers over me, then stops immediately.

"Fuck, I don't have any condoms on me. I've been so messed up, I forgot to grab some from the loft." In this moment, I don't care if he uses a condom or not. I want him. I want all of him, so I take a chance.

"I'm on birth control and I was checked for STDs last month before we started to be intimate. I'm clean." He looks down at me and in that moment, I'm scared as shit at what he might say.

He pulls me in and gives me a hug I never thought he could actually do. And he just holds me and holds me until…

"You are driving me crazy, Lily. I've been wanting you for a long time, I just never said anything. I know we work together, and I don't want things to be—"

"I like you too, Jason, but you do know that we can't be anything more than this, right?"

He physically tenses and I want to take it back, but we can't be more than what we are now. He then smashes his lips to mine and devours me like he didn't hear what I just said. Like it is the first time he's ever kissed me, and I open up to him willingly. I drop the conversation and I give him all of me and he gives me all of him in this very moment. He lays me down on my bed and spreads my legs with his.

"Yes, I know. I'm clean too, but understand once we do this, it's just me and you. No one else." I nod my head as a response. "Answer me," he commands.

"Yes, I understand. Just you and me." He swipes his fingers over my clit and I nearly fall apart. I hear a deep grunt from within his chest and he inhales all of my essences.

"Fuck, you are so wet for me. You smell so fucking good. I need you now." He thrusts his large dick inside of me and I immediately scream out and arch my back off the bed. He pushes me down and thrusts over and over again.

"Ah, you feel so good. Please, baby, harder, please." And at that very moment, he gives me what I want. He fucks me hard and rough. I need it hard and rough. I need to forget, for just a moment, about the rest of the world. Just as I feel tingles in my feet spreading throughout my body, he pulls out and for a moment I feel lost. He then dives between my legs and eats the fuck out of me, pulling my orgasm out of me.

"Yes, come for me, Butterfly. Give it to me, give me all of you. I want to taste you." I place my hands in his hair and I push his mouth deeper inside of me. He is penetrating me with his tongue and then I finally release the biggest orgasm I've ever felt.

"Oh, god, Jason. Oh, god."

"Yes, baby. My butterfly. Give it to me." He stops his assault as the wave of utopia disappears. He then thrusts his dick back inside my pussy. He is balls deep inside of me and I feel him stretching me. But I don't give a damn about the pain. I need the pleasure. I grab his ass and rock with him for a deeper feel.

"God, I feel you in my stomach. Baby, please don't stop." This is so much better without a condom. I didn't think sex could get any better. I can make love to Jason every day—wait—make love? Yes, make love to the man I love. I will never admit that, but I can't deny how I feel. I can keep my thoughts to myself. It's too soon and I don't want to scare this sex god away. I need him.

"Butterfly, open your eyes. I want to see you come for me."

I open my eyes and at that moment, I feel the need, the desire from this man, my man. "I want to feel you come inside of me, please." I reach up with my palm and touch his face. He continues to rock inside of me, hitting my g-spot repeatedly. I feel my body tense and at that moment, I don't give a damn about anything else, but the man giving me all of him.

"I'm about to come, Butterfly."

"Yes, give it to me. I want to feel you." He thrusts one more time and releases all of his essence inside me. I feel his dick throbbing inside, vibrating my walls, filling me up with all of him. It's so much, I feel it run down my ass and onto the bed. It's the best feeling I ever felt.

"You feel so good, Jason."

"You do too, Butterfly." He grunts when he is finished, completely out of breath, and places a kiss on my forehead and rolls over to hold me.

"Butterfly, you are fucking incredible. I had no idea it could feel this good to have sex with you without a condom."

"Those were my thoughts as well. I know you are concerned about us working together, but I know we will figure things out. I want to keep working and doing the very thing I love to do other than fuck my boyfriend."

"Boyfriend, huh? I like the sound of that. I'm Lily's boyfriend and Lily is my girlfriend." We both laugh. Wow, it's been a long time since I've laughed. It feels good.

We both lie still and quiet in each other's arms for a little while. We don't realize we drift to sleep until I hear my phone ringing. I roll over to get it. It's Amelia.

I answer the phone. "Hey, Amelia."

"Hey, sis. Dianella and I received a call from Detective Knight to come straight home. Is everything okay?"

Shit, I forgot to call my sister to let her know what was going on.

"Yes and no. We received some compelling evidence that the killer may be closer to me than I thought. We are trying to figure it out, but for now I want you and Dianella to stay at the loft until then. Can you do this for me?"

"Oh my gosh. Of course. We will stay at the loft. We can work remotely from the loft and work the café."

"Thank you, Amelia, for understanding."

"Absolutely. Are you okay, Lily?"

"Yes, I'm okay." Lying has never been my strong suit unless I am working, but she doesn't push me on it. She knows deep down I am terrified. Not for me, but for her. If anything happens to me, she will have no one, and that terrifies me more than anything. I always have her best interest at heart, and she will always be my beneficiary unless I ever get married, which I'm not.

"I love you, Lily."

"I love you too, sis, and I will see you soon. We are just working on this case and it will take a lot of my time." I feel the tears rolling down my face and at that moment I realize I am crying. Not for me, but for my sister. I hang up the phone and I feel Jason pull me into his arms.

"Let it out, Lily. I will always be here to protect you. Always." All of a sudden, I cry like a baby, a really nasty, ugly cry. And he just holds me and rocks me and comforts me in my time of need. He then kisses my tears and tells me over and over…

"I'm here, Lily."

He catches me off guard by his confession. I pretend I didn't hear it. I love him, but am I ready to say it out loud? There's a whole lot I do not know about him and there is a lot he doesn't know about me.

I get out of his embrace and I head to my safe and grab the thumb drives while Jason washes off in my bathroom. I need to speak to my therapist. I have so many emotions, I'm not sure what to make of them all. Jason has always made me happy, but am I allowed to be happy when there are girls being killed; when this psycho may be after me? I'm not sure if I should be angry or happy. I put my thumbprint on the safe and open it up. Dad always taught me to be extra careful with all my important property. I just didn't know how important until now. I reach for the shoe box I keep them in and open it up. There are over one hundred thumb drives. Good thing I have OCD and labeled them by date and color for each person. Who would have thought this would come in handy? I walk out of the closet and find Jason coming out of the bathroom looking all sexy.

"Here are the thumb drives. They are all color-coordinated and labeled by dates."

He looks in the shoe box and his eyes get wide. "Wow, these are a lot of thumb drives. Do you record everything and everyone?"

"Only when I get their permission. Most people forget I'm even recording them. I know it's weird, but—"

"Nonsense. You lost your memory. I completely understand why you do this. I was just surprised at how many they were."

"Well, to be honest, there should only be twenty for Officer Page. I only knew him for three months. I can record up to three days on each thumb drive."

"Sounds like we are going to have a long night. You take half and I will take half."

"Wow, you're willing to listen to my recordings?"

"Of course. We are in this together. I told you. I will do anything to protect you."

"But what if you don't like some of the stuff we are talking about?"

"I'm a big boy. I can take it."

"Okay, don't say I didn't warn you." I hand him over ten thumb drives, a pair of AirPods, and a MacBook Pro. We start listening to the first set of recordings.

First Recording

> *Hi, Matthews and your name?*

> *My name is Anthony.*

Is that your first or last name?

Is Matthews your first or last name?

Point taken, my name is Lily Matthews and yours?

Anthony Page. Your name fits you.

Yeah, how so?

You come off as motherly, pure of heart, passion and drive, renewal and rebirth.

You got all that in one conversation?

I read people very well.

So do I, but I'm not barbaric about it.

So, you think I'm barbaric?

No, I didn't say that, but you are arrogant, reserved, a little shy at times which can be a calming attribute to your personality.
You usually keep your opinion to yourself and try not to impose emotional influence on other people, but I see you are not that way with me. Who would have thought?

Could it be that I find you intriguing?

Possibly, but not likely.

Why do you think that?

I'm nothing special. I come to work, give it my all, and then go home. See, nothing special over here.

I would have to disagree, but okay.

"On this recording, we were pretty much getting to know each other as partners. It's crazy how I forgot all about this conversation. We got into greater details of our lives I think a week or two after our initial contact."

Recording Three

> Hey, Matthews. Let's get the pool car and head out. We have a call pending.

> Sure, I have to grab something out of my locker, and I will meet you at the car.

> Okay.

> Hey, Page, I want to ask you something. You don't have to answer if you don't want to, but I want to ask anyway.

> Okay, shoot.

> Do you think you are a reserved person because you don't want to complicate things in your life?

Wow, where did that come from?

A conversation we had the other day had me thinking about myself.

Well, I find comfort in being selective about the information I share with other people and who I share it with.

I can understand that, but I find it difficult for me to remember things because of my past and I do not want to be this way anymore.

Well, you cannot force yourself to be something you are not familiar with. I find that being reserved; it means I have a high sense of self-awareness and I don't give people much of an opportunity to judge or label me. My independence allows me to make my own decisions without consulting others or family.

Why would you want to keep things from your family?

Not all of us grew up with a happy ending or beginning for that matter. It was very hard for me and my family at times. I just chose a different path than some.

I get that. My sister is everything to me. I would protect her from anything, but in the end, she is my best friend. I share my deepest secrets with her.

I have a brother. But I wouldn't trust him further than I can throw him. We are completely different, and I like it that way.

I guess I never thought about it that way. But I also could not imagine my sister out of my life.

Well, you haven't met my brother and you don't want to.

"He has a brother. That is what we are missing."

"What do you mean, Lily?"

"The DNA we found may explain something more than what we found. I need to speak to Officer Day."

Chapter 13

Jason

I dial the office number and have Knight patch us through to Forensics. Lily is on to something, but we want to verify if it is even possible before we confront Officer Page. She is always thorough, and she forces me not to jump to conclusions so quickly. I love that about her. Wow, who would have thought I would have fallen in love with someone. Not me in a million light-years would I have thought this was coming. But it has come and now I don't need to screw it up. Officer Day answers the phone.

"Officer Day."

"Hi, Officer Day, this is Detective Hall. I have a couple of questions for you."

"Okay, shoot."

"Is it possible for siblings or family members to have the same DNA?"

"Yes and no. And here is why. Siblings can and do have different DNA. Siblings share roughly 50 percent of their DNA with each other, but it depends on how their chromosomes are randomly assorted. When people are related, they share kinship with the other person and are descended from the same common ancestor. This is also true for identical twins. Because identical twins have the same DNA, it is nearly impossible to distinguish between these individuals when analyzing DNA for paternity testing or for evidence of a crime. The question becomes, could identical twins pull off the perfect crime? The answer is yes, they could. Would they? Well, that is a question you must find out. I just provide the science. You apply the science to solve the crime. Either way, I will be here to explain it all in the court of law."

"Thanks, Officer Day. I appreciate the help. I'm not sure, but I think I'm on to something with this case. Thanks again and take care."

"No problem. I'm always here to help." The phone disconnects.

Holy shit, Page has a twin. Who the fuck would have thought that?

"Holy shit, Officer Page has an identical twin, doesn't he?" asked Knight. She pulls the question right out of my head.

"I'm not completely sure about that," Lily says. "He did say he had a brother and he hated him with all his being. At the time, I didn't understand it, but now I think I do. In some of the recordings Page talks about how he grew up in a different world than the rest of us. What if he grew up in an abusive home? What if he and his brother suffered a problem with bullying in school or at home? What if they had an overcontrolling mother who projected physical and emotional abuse? There are so many factors that we must have answered, and I know just how to get them."

"Oh no, the fuck you will. I'm not letting you go near that psycho by yourself."

"You really don't have a choice, Jason, and I'm doing this whether you like it or not. Page listens to me. He respects me. He will not talk to you or anyone else. I have to do this alone. If you want to be my fucking savior, then put a wire on me and listen in."

She is really fucking pushing me to my fucking limit.

"Fine, Knight, get her a wire, because she will not walk out this fucking office without us being within five seconds of response time. Do I make myself clear?"

"Crystal." Lily rolls her eyes once again. I don't think she realize how that turns me on.

"Gotcha, boss," says Knight.

I walk out the conference room, slam the door, and go into my office. I am so fucking furious right now. I don't know why she insists on pissing me off. I feel an overwhelming need to bend her over my desk and fuck her hard and rough. I am so fucking hard right now. I can't believe this asshole is putting my girl into harm's way.

"Fuck you, Page." Yelling more to myself than to anyone else.

How can I just sit back and let the love of my life walk into the deep end of the firepit? Because I am her partner first at work and her lover second at home. This is bullshit. My door opens and just like that my anger has disappeared.

"Are you okay?" Lily asks.

"No, I'm not okay. But do I have a fucking choice?"

"Actually, yes you do. I am not used to having someone care this much about me and I was wrong for putting you in that position." She reaches out to me and I respond immediately. She wraps her arms around my waist and places her head on my chest and I instantly melt in her arms. All I want to do is keep her safe and I want her to understand how much I need to keep her safe.

"I want to, no, I need to protect you at all cost. I just got you and I don't want to lose you. Not now, not ever."

"I get it now. I will not put myself in harm's way, but understand, we have a job to do and I know I can get what we need out of Page and I know I have to do this on my own. Do you understand that?" She looks up at me with those big, beautiful eyes. How can I deny her anything?

"I understand, but you understand, I will not let you out of my sight the entire time you are with this guy."

"Deal." She smiles the most gorgeous smile I have ever seen, and I place a soft kiss on her lips, letting her know who she belongs to. She belongs to me and I will never let her forget that.

Chapter 14

Lily

I take a deep breath, "Lily, you can do this," I say to myself.

"Yes, Lily, you got this."

Shit, I forgot I was being monitored. I take a few more deep breaths and walk into The Grind.

I search for Page. It feels a little weird that I am meeting another guy in my boyfriend's coffee shop. I find him sitting in the back of the café sipping on a cup of coffee. He waves his hand, gesturing for me to come over. As I walk over, Maggie asks me if I want a cup of coffee.

"Yes, I would love a cup with cream and sugar please. Thank you."

"Coming up."

"How have you been, Page?"

"I could be better, Lily. I'm glad you called. I kind of miss riding with you. You never know what you have until it's gone." He looks so defeated. I actually feel sorry for him.

"I know I've been so tied up on this case and haven't really had free time. I would like to talk to you about a couple of things. Are you up to it?"

"Of course."

Here goes nothing.

"We've come to some leads in the case and have questions about it and you may be able to help."

"How can I help? What does this have to do with me?" He visibly tenses up.

"Well, we think the killer may be a photographer, or may be going to school for photography. Do you know of anyone who could possibly help us?"

"I'm not sure. I would have to think about—wait, I do know some people."

"Really, that's great. We thought about contacting every photographer in Savannah, but then came to the conclusion that this person may not publish himself as a photographer. He may be working behind the scenes or working with someone else." I pull out my notebook, ready to write down the names. I don't want him to become suspicious of me recording him.

"Does it matter that some of these people I know may be women?" he asks.

"No, it doesn't matter. I look through every possible lead."

"That you do. I'm actually surprised you called me for help."

"Why are you surprised about that? You have always helped me understand what was going on in my head when I was overwhelmed with details and you know more about photography than I do. Why not come to you?"

"You got a point there. I just thought you would reach out to your new boy toy." Shocked, I look up at him ready to pounce, but then— "I didn't mean it that way. I just meant you have a new partner to sift through all the BS and get to the point."

"Well, to set the record straight, I don't have boy toys. I fuck who I want to fuck and when I am done with him or her, I'm done. That's not playing with toys, that's getting a fix and moving on. "So, fuck you for indicating that I can't do the same damn thing as any other man in this world." I've had it with boys thinking that just because I am a woman, I need to carry myself a certain way. Fuck anyone who would belittle my worth. "And how the fuck do you know who I fuck and don't fuck? I don't actually fuck and share with you."

"I don't know. I just assumed—"

"Assumed that I was a slut and fucked anything that walks without a care in the world? That assumption? You know what, just forget about it. I am so tired of people judging me. I'm just like anyone else in this fucking city. I like to have fun too. So, fuck you for even suggesting I'm beneath you."

"Lily, no, it's not like that. How do you not know that I like you? I've always liked you. You just treated me like a partner and that's it."

Blown away, I respond the only way I know how. "You are my partner. I can't have a relationship with my partner. You know that."

"Do I? Do you?"

"What are you implying?"

"We aren't partners anymore. So, what's stopping you now?"

"Because I am in a relationship now. Yeah, a real relationship. If you wanted me, you should have said something a long time ago. Now can we drop this and get back to the case?" I refuse to let him know the real reason I never saw him like that.

"Yes, sorry I pissed you off. That was not my intention. I just wanted you to know, you have options." Dropping the conversation, he gives me names of people who are underground photographers. "Tracy Johnson, Paul Wright, Joseph Wilson, John Carter all work from their apartments. They usually post on Instagram, Twitter, or Facebook. Oh, wait, I forgot one more person, but he wouldn't—"

I put my pen down and look up. "Who is the last person?"

"Well, you remember I told you I had a fucked-up family?" I nod, encouraging him to continue. "Well, I never really talked about my siblings." Fuck, he has more than one sibling. "I have two other brothers, Adam and Andrew, and a sister, Abby. My brothers and I are triplets. My mother was a psychopath to our older sister. Like really crazy to our older sister. Our mom used to tie her to the bed and beat her until she saw blood and force her to fuck her boyfriends for money. Our mom was fucking twisted in the head. My sister eventually was able to run away, but then my mom got pregnant with triplets. My sister found out about it and returned home. She wanted to protect us as much as possible from our crazy mother. Once my mom had us, we were immediately taken away and we were placed in foster care. My sister just turned eighteen and was determined to get full custody over us. Once she was rewarded custody five years later, two of our brothers started showing signs of personality disorder, bipolar syndrome, and psychopathic behavior. They hated our mother and hated our sister for not getting us sooner. She did everything in her power to erase the horrible behaviors, but they were too much to handle. She decided to have them committed in a psych ward. They never forgave her for that. I am the only one out of my brothers who did not inherit our mother's disorders. In fact, I sent myself to therapy just in case. I am everything you said I was only because I don't want people to judge me for my family's past. Anyway, that is why I became a police officer. I know it's crazy, but there it is. My truth."

For the first time in my life, I am speechless. This explains so much and I am just trying to process it. "Wow, I had no idea."

"No one had any idea. I keep to myself for a reason."

"So, let me get this straight. You have two other brothers who are triplets with you and an older sister who is eighteen years older than the three of you. Correct?"

"Yes, that's correct."

"When you were in foster care, where did y'all go if you don't mind me asking?"

"No, not at all. We all went to Greenbriar. To this day I donate money to Greenbriar to help with the kids who are stuck in that hellhole. I plan on adopting someday as well. I just feel like I can do more."

"I get it. Like I really get it. Do you know where your brothers are now?"

"I found out yesterday that they both were released. I've been trying to track them down all day."

"How long have they been released?"

"Three months."

Fuck, that's around the time the killings started.

"When was the last time you heard from your sister?"

"Two weeks ago. I asked Sarge if I could take a couple of personal days, but he wouldn't budge. I was on my way to my sister's house when you called me."

"I am about to tell you something and I just need you to hear me out. Can you do that for me?"

"I think so. What is it?"

"We—" I am about to reveal the rest of our case details when Jason walks in the café. What is he doing?

"Hey, Detective Hall. How are you doing?" I say, giving him a look of disdain. I can handle myself. He really needs to back off.

"I came looking for you. You didn't answer your phone, so I decided to grab a cup of joe and head to your house. I don't have to make the trip after all." He looks furious. But I downplay it.

"Page and I were just having a cup of coffee and talking. Would you like to join us?"

"No, actually we have some leads on the case. I need you to come to the office. I hate to break up this intimate little moment."

Asshole.

"No moment here." I look at him with death daggers in my eyes. He knows I am not letting this go.

"Matthews, go ahead. I have to head out of town anyway. I just didn't want to ignore your phone call."

"Okay Page, I will talk with you soon."

He gets up, throws twenty bucks on the table, looks at Jason, and walks out of the café.

"Rude much?"

"No, we are having Knight tail him so we can figure out what's going on. I didn't want you to reveal the rest of our case because we do not know yet if we can trust him. He may very well be a part of all this."

"I get it, but I don't think he is. But I will do it your way since I am way too involved in this. Did you hear what he said?"

"Yes, I heard everything. Don't let this steer you from learning the truth. Psychopaths have a way of twisting the truth to fit their truth and your truth."

"He spent time in Greenbriar just like my sister. Just like all the other victims. I never told him that information."

He takes the lapel pin off my shirt and disables the sound. He then pulls me into a hug. I feel overwhelming relief, gratitude that this man is in my life. This case has become a part of who I am and what I am about. He is the only one who has the power to calm me down.

"Butterfly, baby. I'm here. You will get through this. We both will together." His phone pings with a message. "Page is on the move. Knight is behind him. We should go."

I wipe my face with a paper towel while Jason hides me from the public. He is giving me time to clean up myself before I walk back into the world of uncertainty.

"Okay, I'm ready."

He gives me a quick kiss on the forehead, and we walk out together. I see Maggie in the corner of my eye. She looks so pissed right now. Well, I don't know how she feels right now, but I can certainly guess. He is an amazing guy and he is mine. All mine. I look at her with empathy in my eyes and she looks away intimidated and hurt.

Chapter 15

Jason

The hardest thing I've ever had to experience is listening to another man poach my girl. I knew there was something there, but actually hearing it pissed me off. It took my entire being to sit there and listen to that shit. And then for him to degrade my butterfly like she was some kind of whore was the end of the straw. Knight had to literally sit on top of me to stop me from storming in my fucking café and putting a bullet in his head. But Knight convinced me that Lily had it. She could handle herself and she did. Very well. I knew it was hard for her to sit there and listen to all of those confessions and not break down, but she held it together like a pro. I can see why she is attached to him, but now I know she is not in love with him like she is with me, even though she has not said it yet. She loves him, but like a brother, a partner more so than a lover. That is the only reason I haven't gone apeshit on everyone.

We decided to take my SUV because this is going to be a long road trip. Knight is giving us updates so we can keep up with her. She is about thirty minutes ahead of us. Lily leans her seat back and closes her eyes. I think this is really taking a toll on her and when this is all over, I am taking her somewhere relaxing and soothing for the both of us. We both need it, but she needs it more than I do. I even thought about bringing our sisters with us. Make it a family trip. I think that would be a great idea.

I notice that we seem to be heading for the Florida-Georgia state line. I send Knight a text.

> Have you entered Florida?

>> Yes, it looks like we are headed for Amelia Island.

> Are you fucking kidding me?

>> Nope, just took the exit. Did you speak to your sister and Amelia yet? Just to make sure they are okay?

> Yes, they are both okay.

>> Just making sure. This case is getting weirder by the second.

Yes, I know.

I will let you know when we come to a stop.

Received.

Lily wakes up, stretching her limbs because it must be uncomfortable sleeping in a car. She looks so breathtaking when she first wakes up. She does this little twitch with her nose. It's the cutest thing I've ever seen.

"Good morning, sunshine."

"Good morning—wait—is it morning already? How long did I sleep? Where are we?"

"Slow down with the questions, good grief. It's not morning. I was just quoting a movie. You were only sleeping for two hours and we've just crossed the Georgia-Florida state line."

"What, we're in Florida?"

"Yes, apparently we are headed to Amelia Island." The color drains out of her face, her eyes are stretched wide open, and she has stopped breathing. I grab her thigh to let her know that I am still here, and she begins to breathe again.

"I'm okay. I just—I just don't get this. What does all of this have to do with me and my sister?"

"I don't know, but we will figure this out."

"Amelia Island of all places in the world," she says more to herself than me.

"We are about to take the exit to the beach. Are you up for this?"

"Absolutely, I need to know what's going on."

"Good, that's my girl."

Located just off the coast of northeast Florida, Amelia Island is easy to reach, but hard to forget. With thirteen miles of beautiful beaches, abundant native wildlife, and pristine waters, their barrier island has long been a beloved destination for visitors and residents alike. We drive a couple of miles on US-17 in Nassau County when I get a text from Knight.

> *We just pulled up to the Ritz-Carlton resort.*

> *I will wait in the parking lot until you get here. If I notice anything, I will let you know.*

> *Received. We are twenty minutes out.*

"Knight just confirmed that he pulled up to the Ritz-Carlton resort."

"Wow, I didn't know Page had that kind of money."

"Don't always judge a book by its cover. People spend their fortunes very differently."

"Yeah, I guess you are right. Look at us two. Who would have thought we were very wealthy as well?"

Twenty minutes later, we pull up to the Ritz-Carlton. I search for Knight's unmarked vehicle. She is parked in the middle of several other cars. She exits the vehicle and climbs into my backseat.

"Hey y'all," Knight says.

"Hey, Kim. How's it going?"

"I could be home sipping on a mojito, but here I am chasing after bad guys once again."

We can't help but laugh. I mean a real deep-throat, hard, ugly laugh. I hear Knight and Lily snort and they start laughing harder.

"I needed that. Thanks, Kim," says Lily.

"Anytime, my sweet pea." They both look at each other and silently understand the need for each other. It is a special moment to see between them.

We start watching the front entrance and after what seems like forever, we see Page's vehicle pulling up to the front entrance.

"It looks like he is about to head out again."

"Yes, I see—wait. He is with someone. It looks like a woman."

"Could it be his sister?" Knight asked.

"No, his sister is much older than him. It looks like a girl in her late teens, early twenties."

"I wonder who she is? Let's follow him."

"Okay, Knight, stay here and book our rooms. I've already cleared it with the captain. Here is a credit card. Go buy any essentials you need. Don't worry about the cost. I will take care of everything. Do you still have the tracking device I gave you?" I asked.

"Yes, I have it."

"Good, keep it on you at all times."

"Absolutely. I will monitor the cameras once you set them up. And remember, be safe, not stupid."

"Ten-four."

I've always felt a compelling need to make sure my officers are doing okay. Knight lives by herself and I check on her every once in a while. She was involved in a bad relationship and she hasn't been the same since. She has come around a lot better than before, though. She was always bitter and snapped on everyone who came two feet near her. She wanted her space and I respected that. I remember the day I found her half dead on the side of the road. Her ex just beat the shit out of her and left her for dead. I was able to get her to the hospital and save her before she lost too much blood. Ever since then, we've been like sister and brother through everything. I let her live in one of my condos until she was able to get back on her feet. I told her she could stay as long as she wanted, but she refused.

She wanted her independence back and I understood that. That asshole took everything from her, and she claimed it all back slowly but surely. He came looking for her on a number of occasions, but I never let him get close to her. I protected her and she didn't even realize it. I even started a bank account for her. I just haven't told her about it. She would probably kill me.

"What tracking device are you talking about?" asks Lily, cutting through my train of thought.

"I give all my officers tracking devices so we will know each other's location at all times. It keeps us safe."

"Do I get a tracking device?"

"Yes, I just haven't talked to you about it yet."

"Well, now is as good as any other time."

"Touché. Here, hold your wrist out." She holds her wrist out and I place a bracelet around her wrist. "This is a tracking device. It is waterproof; therefore, you never have to take it off."

"Cool, it actually looks pretty. Thank you."

"You're welcome." I pull out my phone to activate the tracker.

"Hey, Jason, he's on the move," Lily says.

I activate the tracker and head out of the parking lot of the Ritz-Carlton. Even though it's nine o'clock in the evening, there is a ton of traffic out. I never realized how busy it is here during tourist time. We are about four car lengths behind Page.

"It's gorgeous here. I forgot how beautiful it is on this island," Lily says.

"You've been here before?" I ask.

"Yes. I forgot about it, but we used to come here every year for my sister's birthday. She looked forward to it every year. They didn't come the night my parents died because I couldn't make it. I had a huge lab project to present and could not join them. They didn't want to go without me, so they stayed in town. If only I could have made it, my parents—"

"Don't do that. It's not your fault. You can never determine the future, but you can pave the way of the present. Your parents are in good hands now. Just remember that, okay?"

"Yes, I know. But sometimes I can't help but wonder."

"If you chase after what ifs, you will drive yourself crazy. There is always a reason for everything. Your parents died and your sister lived for a reason. God only knows that reason."

"You believe in God?" she asks.

Making a right turn at the light, we are still four car lengths behind Page.

"It took me a while to find him again after my history, but my foster mother is the one who guided me towards the Bible and then towards church. She taught me that God is our savior and to put all your faith and trust in him."

"Wow, we never really went to church, but I always believed there was a higher power out there and we needed to respect it."

"Maybe you can come to church with me and Dianella someday."

"I will think about it." I wasn't trying to convert her, but I know she is looking for more in this lifetime and I think she will be able to find it in the Bible. It helped me, maybe it can help her. "Looks like we are headed towards one of the beaches."

"Yes, I think you are right. We must stay out of sight so once it looks like he is about to pull into a house or parking lot, we will keep going straight and then walk towards the area."

"Okay, sounds good to me. I'm just ready for this to be over with," I say.

"Same here." Sure enough, Page pulls onto a dirt road headed to a house settled on the beach.

"Lily, send Knight the address so she can pull the records of the owner."

"Absolutely." She sends Knight a text message and it seems like seconds when Knight responds back.

Lily reads the text and says, "The owners of the property are Anthony and Abbey Page. They have owned the property for ten years. Knight also ran the sister's information. It states that she has no record, not even parking tickets. All her debts are paid off and she doesn't work. She gave birth to a girl twenty years ago and that child's name is Alexandra Page. There is no father listed. It appears that Anthony sends them money every month and quite a bit of money. He sends ten thousand dollars each month and set up a college fund for his niece. Wow, Knight is good."

"Yes, that is why I snatched her up out of the academy. She is very good at hacking and discovery."

"Yes, she is very good at what she does," Lily replies.

Both Page and the young lady get out of the car. We snap pictures of the encounter and send them to Knight to process them. An older woman, in her late forties walks out the front door and gives the young girl a hug and a kiss and then she embraces Page. A man steps out the house and for a second I have to do a double take. The man is the spitting image of Page. It must be one of the triplets. Page draws his weapon and points it at the man. The man raises his hands as he is surrendering to Page. The man walks toward Page, who fires a warning shot.

"Oh fuck, we have to do something."

I pull Lily back. "We are not engaging. We are only observing."

"He just shot at his brother. That alone is aggravated assault."

"There is more to this story. If we interfere now, we will not get the answers we need."

"I get it, but how do we just sit here and watch him commit a crime?"

"Easy, like this." I snap a couple of more pics and send them to Knight.

"I'm not used to this stake-out stuff."

"That is why I am here to guide you. You will get used to it soon enough."

"We shall see."

Page, the two women, and one of the other triplets all enter the house.

Chapter 16

Lily

After what seems forever, Page heads back to the hotel with us following four car lengths behind. Never in a million years would I have thought I would be in a car with Detective Jason Hall staking out my partner, Officer Anthony Page. If someone would have told me this months ago, I would have laughed in their face. But now, I feel I am right where I should be. I'm still blown away that Jason even considers being with me. At first, I was going to haul ass out the door and never look back, but then something told me not to be afraid of love anymore. I should tell him how I feel, but I don't think I'm there yet. Not yet. But I also need to embrace it and understand that I can be loved by someone else other than my sister.

I turn to look at Jason, like really look at him. He is absolutely stunning. He could be with anyone in this world and he chose me. There are so many other beautiful women out there. I see them staring when we are at crime scenes and I even noticed it when we all were at the bar the other night. But he only has eyes for me, little ole me.

"Why me?" I ask loudly without even thinking.

"What do you mean?"

"Why do you care so much about me? You can have any woman in the world. Why me? Why did you choose to be with me?"

"Well, to be honest, I never thought I could or would be with someone like you. I had a conversation the other day with my sister and she basically said I was wasting my life away. You are right, I could have any woman I want. I've had many before I met you, but since we've been together, you are the only thing I think of when I wake up in the morning and the last thing I think about when I go to sleep at night. You are the most beautiful woman I've ever seen and more. You don't need me for my money, but you want me for me. The hardest thing I ever had to endure was sitting there listening to someone else profess their love for you. I know this is still new for both of us, but I want to try, and I am willing to do anything to keep you in my life. You don't have to feel it back, but to be honest, I'm hoping you feel the same way or will in time."

After that answer, I become rigidly still and lose my way of speaking. I know I asked the question, but I was not expecting that answer. I need to say the words. He needs to hear how I feel about him too.

"I don't know what to say. I've never experienced this before. All I know is I feel the same way and don't ever think I can lose you either. But I'm terrified." I've never been much of a crier, but lately I find myself crying all the time. It makes me feel so weak.

"Butterfly, I am not expecting you to change the world overnight. I know what I want, and I will not stop until I get it. I am willing to be patient and wait until the moment comes to have you all to myself."

I am floored by that response. "So are you saying I'm a quest that you must complete and once you're done, you're done with me?"

"Fuck no, that's not what I meant. I'm just saying that I am a determined and confident person and I wanted to do everything in my power to let you know that I am the man for you. I know you don't need my money, but I want to give you everything. I know you don't need my security, but I find myself protective over you. I know you don't need me, but I am hoping that you do."

"I'm sorry. I am really on edge and don't mean to take it out on you."

"It's okay. That is what I am here for, to help you through this and be there to support you whenever you need me."

That's the sweetest thing he could have said to me. We arrive at the hotel but wait inside the car until Page makes it to his room. Knight found out which room is his and set up surveillance inside. Jason grabs my hand and links our fingers together. He looks into my eyes and for the first time, I see vulnerability. He is scared just like I am. I stroke his hand with my fingers to remind him that I am here with him. I know he needs me just as much as I need him.

"Jason, you don't always have to put on a brave face for me either. I know you need guidance and reassurance as well as I do. You can talk to me about anything."

"I know."

Knight sends me a message stating that we are clear to head to our room.

> *Wait, did you just get one room?*

> > *Yes, of course. Why wouldn't I?*

> *Because it is inappropriate to stay in one room.*

> > *Oh, please. I know y'all are fucking. Drop the act. And besides, I won't tell anyone. I got you.*

Flabbergasted, I look at Jason for whatever support he can provide. I don't want our personal life to affect our professional life. I need this job. I desire this job.

"I know what you are thinking. It will be okay. I will never allow our personal life to affect our work. If you want me to get another room, I will. I respect you and I will do whatever you want me to do."

The ball is in my court and I don't want to make the wrong decision. I want him in my bed so bad, but if someone questions why I wasn't in a different room, it will be a bad day for the both of us.

"I think we should get separate rooms. Not because I don't want to sleep with you, but because this is work related and I don't want anyone to question us."

"I get it. I will book another room."

Chapter 17

Jason

The second hardest thing I had to do in my life was watch the love of my life enter a different room. For a minute there I wanted to force her to stay in my room, but I knew I could not do that. I have to respect her decision. She has a lot to lose and I don't want to be responsible for her losing everything she worked so hard for. I will never betray her.

I decide to text Knight so she can bring me my bag. She purchased us some toiletries and a change of clothes. I didn't have to tell Knight what I needed because we have done this plenty of times before while staking out. She texts back saying she is on her way. Seconds later I hear a knock on the door.

"Hold on, I'm coming." I go to open the door and find Knight standing there with two bags. I grab the bags and let her in the room.

"Where is Lily?"

"She is in her room." Knowing that she is about to flood me with questions, I answer all her unspoken words. "We are working, and it would be inappropriate for us to sleep in the same room."

"Who the hell will find out?"

"No one, but that is not the point. I respect her decision, so just drop it." I know she wants to say more, but she listens and drops the conversation.

"So, I've been listening to the surveillance I put in Page's room," she says. "From the conversations he has been having on the phone with his sister and his niece, it sounds like he can't find one of his brothers. All three of them have been looking. The third brother won't give up his location, so Page is trying to track him down himself. I really believe he cares about Lily and will do anything to get her."

That little statement just infuriates me. I think Knight notices my body language change and tries to retract her statement.

"I…I didn't mean it that way. I…just think Lily is his motivation to find the crazy guy and we will need him. Let him do the work and we surveil him. That's all I meant by that statement. Jeez, don't rip my head off."

"I'm not mad at you. I just hate this guy. I had a bad vibe about him since the day I met him. He really comes off weird."

"I get it. Let's use it to our advantage. Anyways, I need to take Lily her stuff. I'm actually surprised she has not asked for it yet."

"Actually, to think of it, I'm surprised by that too. I would have thought she would have texted me by now." I pick up my phone and give her a call. "It went straight to voicemail. She never lets my calls go to voicemail."

"What room is she in?"

"Room 804."

Knight understands what I'm about to do and reaches the door first. We run down the hall and find the door ajar with the stopper stopping the door from closing. I bust through the door and find the room a mess. It looks like a hurricane came through and left its hatred in this one room.

"Lily, Lily? Answer me, baby? Please answer me?"

Knight grabs me by the arm and I almost throw her across the room. She stands her ground and stop me from taking her out.

"Calm down, Hall. We will find her."

"Don't fucking tell me to calm down. I lost the love of my life. I promised her I would keep her safe." My mind is everywhere. I can't think straight. If that asshole does anything to her, I am going to fucking kill him. Venom in every word I spit out.

"Hall, did you give her a tracking device like you gave me?"

Realizing what she just said, I scramble to my feet and grab my phone from my back pocket.

"Yes, I gave her the bracelet earlier just in case. I'm glad I was thinking." I pull up the GPS. Her last known location was heading north on I-95.

"Call the locals and tell them about the kidnapping. Take pictures of the scene. I'm going after her."

"Wait, we need to see if Page is still here. They may be together. He might have taken her."

"You're right." Knight pulls up the surveillance and we both gasp.

"The feed has been cut." Knight heads for the door. "I know which room he was in."

We head to the elevator and take it to the fourth floor. We head down the hall to room 404. What a fuck coincidence that he is in this room. I bang on the door. There is no answer. I then kick in the door. His room looks like shit too. As if there was a struggle. How the fuck are two rooms thrown like this. This is no coincidence. This is a set-up.

"What the fuck? This bastard is trying to play games with me. Knight, do what I say, and I am headed back to Savannah. They are only twenty minutes ahead of me."

"Ten-four."

I head back to my room and leave Knight to do what she does best. I grab my keys and shit and head for the elevators. I get a phone call and I answer immediately.

"Yeah?"

"Now, is that any way to treat the person who has your girlfriend?"

My blood starts to boil and at that moment I think I can actually burst into flames. "If you lay one fucking finger on her, I will kill—"

"Now, now, now, don't make threats you can't keep." This motherfucker is pushing me to my breaking point. "If you want to find your precious love in one piece, you will do as I say." My precious love. He is right. I am in love with Lily and I was such a coward; I never told her how I felt.

Not having any choice in the matter, I let him speak.

"Now, that sounds better. Meet us at The Grind. I want a coffee with my dessert." Then he hangs up.

"Fuck you, asshole," I yell into the phone. I run through the lobby and head for my SUV. This asshole has my baby, my butterfly, the love of my life. God only knows what he is doing to her. Fuck, I can't think like that right now. She is strong. She can handle herself.

"I'm coming, baby, my butterfly."

Chapter 18

Lily

I feel myself waking up. My body is aching all over, like I've been in a fight of a lifetime or hit by a truck. I try to move but my hands are restrained. Wait, my hands are handcuffed. It's dark and I have trouble breathing. Where am I? My first instinct is to scream, but then I hear voices.

Wait, I'm in a trunk of a car. We are moving, but I don't know where. I feel the car bouncing up and down as if we are on a highway.

I hear voices, but I can't make them out. What happened?

Wait, I remember now. I insisted that I get my own room, and now look at me. I should have stayed with Jason. I'm such an idiot. Jason was practically begging me to stay with him with just the intense look in his eyes. I shouldn't have been so weak, so proud, so stupid. Wait...

Fuck, where are Jason and Kim? Are they okay? I need to get out of here.

Think, Lily, think. I always keep a handcuff key in my shoe. I try to reach for my shoes. Damnit. I can't reach it. But I can move my hands in front of me. Thanks to yoga, my flexibility has improved tremendously. I then wiggle my arms in front of me. Yes, I did it.

Now I need to get the handcuff key. People thought I was crazy for doing this, but now I am glad I thought about this. I reach into my shoe and slip my finger into the slot I cut into my shoe. I grab the key as carefully as I can even though I am shaking to death.

I stop for a moment. Take a deep breath. Calm down, Lily. Once I calm down, I curve my wrist so I can put the key in the slot. It enters and I almost lose my mind with anticipation. I turn the key and flex my wrist and fingers to get one of the cuffs off. I'm free. Yes, god damn it. I'm free. I then take the other cuff off and drop the cuffs on the floorboard. I put the key back into my shoe just in case.

I have no idea where I am going, so all I can do is sit here in the trunk. I need to wait until they pull over or get to their destination. I need something to knock one of them out. I feel around for anything I can use. I find a crowbar. This is perfect.

I then check my pockets for my phone. Wishful thinking. They took my phone, bastards. I have no idea where I am going, and I don't have anything to communicate with. I am so fucked right now, but I will not let them kill me without putting up a fight. I need to be strong for Amelia and Jason.

Wait, is Amelia okay? Is Dianella okay? I told them to stay at the loft, but did they listen to me? I just pray that they did.

I feel the vehicle slow down a little, and the bumping has slowed down as well. Where are we going? I need to plan something. I need to brainstorm to get myself out of this.

I go back to how they got me in the first place. Someone pushed me in my room once I opened the door. Jason had already walked into his room. It took him a while because he probably was hoping I would change my mind. I tried to fight back, but someone else came up behind me when I slammed the first guy on the ground. I was about to pull my gun when everything went black. I must have been hit in the head. Almost instantly, I felt pain on the back of my head. Someone was watching me. Someone knew I would be alone.

My mind goes back to Page. After I told him he had no chance to be a part of my life romantically, he must have gotten madder than I thought. Maybe I can charm my way out of this.

Or maybe this is my fate. Maybe it's my time to leave this earth and be with my parents. Oh, how I will feel to see them again. They are my everything. They are my rock, my strength. No, Lily, you can't think like that. You need to be here for Amelia. Amelia will be devastated if anything happens to me. I have to fight back. I will fight back.

The car stops and I hear the doors slam. My heart pounds in my chest, and I start to sweat. I grab the crowbar, ready to kill whoever the hell opens this trunk. Then I hear footsteps heading toward the back of the car. The trunk pops open.

Chapter 19

Jason

I'm driving 150 mph on I-95. Swerving in and out of traffic. I'm surprised no one has tried to stop me yet. Even if they do, I won't stop. Lily needs me and I will be damned if I let anything happen to her. She means everything to me. I love her and I want to marry her. I have to get her back. I continue to look at the GPS. Even though that asshole told me to go to The Grind, I will go wherever that GPS leads me. Fuck him.

My phone lights up with a message. I play the message through my Bluetooth in the SUV.

"Hey, call me. I know you are driving like a madman, but I need you to answer the phone."

Shit, I didn't realize my phone was ringing. I'm so far gone; I had no idea.

"Call Knight," I yell to Siri.

"Calling Knight," Siri tells me.

She picks up on the first ring.

"Sorry, Knight, I didn't realize my phone was ringing."

"I get it. But we have to stay focused. These guys are smart; we need to be three steps ahead of them."

She is right. I want Lily back so bad that I'm not thinking about the bigger picture.

"You're right. Go ahead."

"I think we have been going about this all wrong," Knight says. I am about to interrupt, but she stops me. "Hear me out." I fall silent to listen to what she has to say. "I think they are all in this together."

"What do you mean?"

"I mean the three brothers and the sister are all in this together. And here is why. Lily said her parents were killed by a drunk driver when she was younger. She said it was a young kid who did not die in the crash. Only her parents. I went back to pull the reports for the accident. Lily never noticed before because she lost her memory from the trauma of losing her parents and having to get her sister back from Greenbriar. The kid who is responsible for killing her parents is Andrew Page."

Holy shit, this can't be.

"Knight, are you sure about this?"

"Yes, I'm sure. I read the reports. He is listed as the driver. He went to jail for vehicular manslaughter, but they deemed him unfit to withstand court, so he went to a psychiatric facility. His brother Adam soon joined him for pushing a kid out of a window at school. This news was so devasting for Anthony and his sister that they moved away to start a new life. But I think they were keeping tabs on Lily and Amelia. I think once Anthony found out about Lily joining the force, he joined also. I think he placed himself in a position where he had to be partners with her without her knowing. I think he was obsessed with her, but she wouldn't give him the time of day and he watched her sleep with other people and go on with her life without ever acknowledging him. And because bipolar and schizophrenia are hereditary, he snapped one day and started sending her gifts in the form of dead women who looked like her, dressed like her, smart like her. I really believe he is behind the killings."

"Knight, I think you are on to something here. Lily was saying the same thing, but she never assumed that her partner would be behind this. I have to get to her before he does anything to her. I'm almost in Savannah. I need to call my sister and Amelia to make sure they are okay as well."

"Okay, I've already alerted the captain, and he is sending additional units your way."

"Thanks, Knight, I owe you my life."

"You owe me nothing. You have always been there for me and now it's my time to be there for you. Be safe and know I love you."

"Love you too, Knight." I know Knight isn't in love with me, but she loves me like a brother, and I love her like a sister. She is right, we have been through a lot together and I would do anything for her. I then tell Siri to call Dianella. She picks up the phone on the first ring.

"Jason, are you okay? Knight called and said something happened to Lily."

"Yes, I'm okay, and I'm on my way to find Lily. Just stay in the loft and don't answer for no one. I don't care if it's the police or not. Don't open that door."

"I understand. Please be careful."

"I will. Is Amelia with you?"

"Yes, she is right here."

"Put me on speaker. I want both of you to hear this."

"You are on speaker."

"Okay, get the gun from the master bedroom and the guest bedroom. Dianella, I taught you how to use it. If I'm not the one walking through that door, you shoot. Do you understand me?"

"Yes, I understand."

"Good, I will see you both soon."

"Jason?" asked Amelia. "Please bring my sister back safely."

"I will. I promise." I am making a promise I don't know if I can keep. But I will do everything in my power to save the love of my life.

Chapter 20

Lily

I am staring in the eyes of my abductor. I know the eyes so well. I've seen them every day in my patrol car. I am staring in the eyes of Anthony Page. He tries to grab me by my arm and that is when I catch him off guard and slam the crowbar into the side of his head. He had no idea that I was no longer handcuffed. He falls to the ground and I jump out of the trunk. I then start whaling on his head with the crowbar. Blood splatters everywhere. I continue because I have so much anger bottled up inside of me. I then hear a gun click like a safety is being released. I stop my assault because it is obvious that the person I hit is very dead. I swing my crowbar to hit the person standing behind me. All I can think is fight or die.

I see the same eyes staring at me, but these eyes are more threatening than the last. They consist of hatred and anger. His arm blocks the crowbar as if it doesn't hurt at all. Any other person, I would have broken their arm. This guy is supernatural. He is not human; he can't be. He snatches the bar from my hand and throws it on the ground. He points the gun to my head and at that moment, I know I'm about to die.

A single bullet to the head, an honorable way to die. Now I know what those girls must have felt when they had their final moments. I'm not scared to die; I am scared to leave my sister and Jason. I'm scared that I will never get the chance to tell him I love him, like really love him. I will never get the chance to be there for my sister when she graduates or when she gets married.

I've finally found love and I never told Jason how I felt. I'm scared he will never know how I truly feel about him. He was a breath of fresh air; he challenged me when I needed it and he supported me when I didn't want it.

"Get in the car."

I open my eyes and see the person standing in front of me. Another Anthony Page staring back at me. I wonder who I just killed.

"No." I decide to be defiant instead of cooperating. If I am going to die, then I might as well take my time.

"Get the fuck in the car or I will make you get in."

I decide to move into the car. He seems to want to take me somewhere. "Fine, I will get in the car, but do know, you will not get away with this."

"You mean like I did with all the other girls?" His voice is deep and creepy. I've always had a weird feeling about Page but could not figure it out. I can't believe I thought he was attractive. I can't believe I trusted him. Whether this is him or not, I need to figure out what the hell is going on.

"You haven't gotten away with killing those poor girls. You are fucking sick and twisted."

"A potty mouth, I love it. My dick is getting hard just listening to the disdain you have for me. I knew I was right to save you for last. This is going to be fun." He chuckles like this is some kind of joke.

I get in the car and he proceeds to the driver's side. I could strangle him with his own seat belt, but I want to see this through. I look around because I realize I never tried to figure out where I was. As I search for any type of clue, I notice a sign that says Tybee Island. We are headed for the beach. We drive toward Fort Pulaski. At this time of night, it's dark and secluded out there.

Fort Pulaski is located on Cockspur Island, about fifteen miles away from historic Savannah, Georgia. The monument was named after the Revolutionary war hero Casimir Pulaski and was established as a National Monument by President Calvin Coolidge in October of 1924.

Today the National Park Service strives to protect, restore, and manage the Fort Pulaski National Monument for all people to enjoy. The construction of Fort Pulaski began in early 1829 and was initially overseen by Major Samuel Babcock.

Now I understand the pictures and of the girls dressed in old-fashioned wedding gowns. This nutjob is obsessed with history and it seems like he wants to reenact the scenes.

"Who are you?" I ask.

"You know who I am."

"Actually, I don't know who you are. Why are you killing these girls?"

"Because it is fascinating to watch the life leave a body while fucking them to bliss."

I stop breathing. No, I can't breathe on my own. I'm having a panic attack. Who the fuck wants to fuck a person while they are dying? This is crazy on so many levels. I have to calm down. He wants me to lose my shit. He gets off on it.

I start to control my breathing. I must stay strong if I want to live. I fidget a little with my hands because I don't know what else to do.

"Don't worry, you will enjoy the accommodations I have for you. I set it up especially for you." I taste a little vomit in my mouth, and I force it down. "I've wanted you for a long time and I am finally going to have you."

This sick motherfucker is obsessed with me. "Why me?" I ask.

"Why not you?"

"I'm nothing special."

"I beg to differ. If that was the case, your lover boy wouldn't be falling over himself trying to get you in his bed."

Asshole, he already had me. "So, you want what you can't have?"

"I can always have you."

"If that's the case, why haven't you had me before."

"I like to stalk my prey before I pounce on them."

"You don't see how twisted that sounds."

"Not twisted, extrinsic."

Okay, I'm dealing with a crazy lunatic. I have to get on his level, or he may just take me into the marsh.

I wonder if I grab the wheel, will I be able to swerve the vehicle. Only one way to find out. I reach for the steering wheel and feel strong hands behind me pull me back to the seat. I almost panic because I never realized that someone was in the back seat. I try to pull away, thrashing my arms and feet everywhere. I then feel something stab into my neck and I feel myself getting weak. I can't move; my eyes begin to close, and I can't keep them open. I've been drugged.

Chapter 21

Jason

The GPS stops moving in an isolated area for about twenty minutes and then it starts moving again. I sent the coordinates to Knight so she can give me the exact location. I need to know why they stopped. I hope they didn't figure out that Lily had a GPS on her. Knight responds to me immediately. She is great at technology. I will definitely give her that.

The coordinates show that they are near Tybee Island. I head in that direction. I'm about ten minutes behind them. I pull into the isolated area and my heart is pounding uncontrollably in my chest. I search the area with jittery eyes. I scan over the open field and notice a hump in the open field. I pull toward it and notice that it's a body. *Fuck, please be someone else; anyone else. Please don't be Lily. Please, God, don't let it be Lily.* I walk up to the body and I immediately break down because of all the stress I was under. I feel hot tears running down my face and I can't control them. I look at the body and automatically realize that the body is way too big to be Lily. Thank God. She is still alive. She has to be.

I flip the body over, and I want to look away, but I don't. The face is smashed in so badly, I can't determine who it is. We will need to check dental records. I leave the body there and get back in the SUV. I text Knight and let her know what I found. I then continue to head in the direction of the GPS. It looks like they are headed to Fort Pulaski. I'm about fifteen minutes away.

I'm coming, Lily. I'm coming, my butterfly.

Chapter 22

Lily

"**U**gh, I don't feel so good." I roll over and vomit. Where am I? I try to move my hands, but they won't budge. I look up and I am handcuffed to a post. My vision is so foggy, and I feel so sick. What is wrong with me? I reopen my eyes and look down at my feet. I can't move my feet. My feet are handcuffed to posts as well. I notice that I have no clothes on and I start to panic. I'm tugging and pulling on the handcuffs, but there is no use. I can't move. I look around and through my blurry vision I see flickering lights, like candles placed all around me. I think I am lying on a bed and I see red things scattered all over the bed. I can't make out what it is. I close my eyes again and try to refocus. I can see a little better, but not very much. The red stuff is rose petals scattered everywhere. I smell the hint of my perfume, Lily by Crabtree and Evelyn. It's the perfume my mom gave to me and what she used to wear all the time. How…

"Hi, beautiful." I try to focus on the voice and where it is coming from. "I know you are scared and wonder what is happening. I will explain all of that very soon, but first I just want to absorb every moment of this reunion. You are the most breathtaking woman I've ever encountered. I've had my share of women, but you top all of them."

"Argh." I can't take this anymore. This guy is making me sick to my stomach. *Lily, you have to think. You need to get out of this now.*

"I know you feel a little groggy, but soon enough you will feel only pleasure and excitement."

Stay calm, Lily, you can get through this.

"I...I need some water."

"Anthony, get the lady some water. She needs her strength for what's about to happen to her."

What? Page is here too? I look over to the corner and I see him cowering like a little bitch. How can he stand there and let this happen to me?

I look at him with disdain. I think I am more hurt than angry that he would allow this to happen to me. "Why?" I whisper so low I don't think anyone could hear me.

"Because he wants to fuck you as much as I do. He will get his turn in just a minute. But first, why you?" I close my eyes and take a deep breath. I'm about to be raped and there is nothing

I can do about it. "You are the reason my brother went to that nuthouse in the first place."

"What do you mean?" I begin to scramble through my brain, trying to remember who I arrested in the past. I put a lot of people in jail or the psych ward.

"Well, to be clear, you are not directly responsible, but your family is. See, my brother and I were having a little fun at a bar and probably had too much to drink. Hell, we were just glad we could get in, let alone drink beer all night long. Andrew was driving and I was bullshitting in the passenger seat. We came around a curve and Andrew lost control and slammed head-on with a vehicle. I was thrown out of the car. Anthony here didn't want to come. He was too much of a pussy. Your parents, however, died in the car wreck. They were too weak to stay alive. What pussies."

I can't breathe. I feel like I'm about to throw up again. I can't believe this is happening. This cannot be true. How dare he talk about my parents like that.

In between trying to breathe, I manage to start talking. "How is this my parents' fault and my fault? We did nothing to you. I didn't even know about the accident; I lost my memory of the whole incident."

"It is your fucking fault because if your parents hadn't died, my brother would have never gone to that nuthouse. And now he is dead because of you!" he yells.

"I was protecting myself. Anyone would have done what I did."

"You're right, but everyone pays a price one way or another. It's time for you to pay. When I found out you lost your memory, I wanted to kill you right then and right there, but Anthony here convinced me to let him get to know you first." I look at Anthony now and I am no longer hurt. I'm pissed beyond measure. I want to see him rot in hell. "I found that intriguing, so I let him make a fool of himself. He was trying so hard for you to notice him; planting little notes here and there, but you didn't give him the time of day. Priceless. Bahahaha." Laughing like a hyena, he begins to drag Anthony toward me.

"I originally wanted to fuck you first, but I think it will please me more to watch Anthony boy fuck you while I photograph your most intimate moment."

I pull on the handcuffs, trying to break the post, but I can't. They both approach me, and Anthony is just staring at my naked body. He starts to take his shirt off and then unbutton his pants. I refuse to beg for my life, so I force my mind to slip into a state of calming. Anthony climbs on top of me and looks into my eyes. I look away, wanting this to be over as soon as possible. He becomes hard while staring at me and all I can think about is this guy is about to rape me and I can't do anything about it. He then lowers on top of me and he starts to insert his dick inside of me. I force my body to stay dry because I will not give him the satisfaction. He begins to rock inside of me, and I just close my eyes and pray that he will just kill me. *Please take my life from this world.* I can smell his breath and I want to vomit but have nothing to vomit. My body starts to convulse, and I shake uncontrollably. I feel like I'm having a heart attack. He is still pumping inside of me.

"Ah, you feel so good, Lily, I don't want to stop," Anthony whispers in my ear.

"No, please." Tears fall down my face and onto the bed. My senses are intensified. I hear the splash of each tear.

"That's it, Anthony, give it to her good. Let her know who is boss. She isn't going to want anyone else after you. Fuck her good."

I have never felt so disgusting in my life. I just want to die and drift away. Now I know how all those girls felt when they were in this very position.

"Please stop," I manage to say through clenched teeth.

As if he never heard me, he continues to pump inside of me and then grunts really loud and starts shaking on top of me. I'm motionless. I can't breathe, I can't think. I just want this to be over with. He finally releases and he falls on top of me, squishing me with his weight. He then strokes my hair like I'm supposed to be pleased with his performance. When he realizes that I don't give a damn about him or anyone else, he turns enraged. He punches me in my face and stomach and I just sit there. I will not give him the satisfaction of being scared or hurt.

"Fuck you, bitch. What does he have that I don't have?"

I refuse to answer him. Another punch in my face. My lip and nose are bleeding. I can taste metallic in my mouth and I know I'm on the verge of passing out and bleeding profusely. *Stay awake, Lily. You are strong.*

"Get the fuck off her. She is mine now." Anthony is pushed to the side so his brother can have his turn with me. Anthony starts to get dressed and his brother starts to undress. I have nothing left in me. I just…just can't anymore. Anthony leaves the room, probably to clean himself up and I lie there to wait for my next assault.

Adam gets on top of me and then gets up. "Shit, I forgot to press play. I am so excited to fuck you; I forget I need to document this. I want to watch later."

Sick to my stomach, I try to vomit again, but I have nothing left in me. It's all gone.

He returns to me and gets on top. He inserts his dick inside of me and grunts deep inside his throat. "Fuck, Anthony is right. You feel so fucking good." He starts to pump inside of me and just as he picks up speed, Anthony comes back in the room. It looks like he saw a ghost.

"Adam, get the fuck up, we have to go. I saw lights outside. Someone is coming."

"Fuck off. I'm not done yet." He continues to pump inside of me harder and harder, faster and faster.

"Hurry the fuck up. We need to go now."

At that very moment he empties inside of me. He gets up and pulls his pants up.

"Next time, I will enjoy you more." He kisses me on the cheek, grabs the camera, and tries to take the handcuffs off me.

"Leave her. We have to go." I start to drift in and out of consciousness and feel relieved that they are giving me a break. The next thing I hear is the door slamming behind them and I am left alone handcuffed to a bed, bloody and naked.

Chapter 23

Jason

I pull up to the fort at Fort Pulaski. Everything is dark, but I see flickering lights coming from one of the windows. I turn the engine off and step out of the vehicle. I pull my duty weapon out and start heading toward the light. I hear voices, but I can't make them out. It sounds like the voices are coming from behind the fort. I then enter the door of one of the rooms. I scan the room to make sure no one is in there. I head down a tunnel-like hallway and start clearing rooms one by one. The GPS shows that Lily is still here, and I am getting closer to her. I pray that she is all right.

With my senses heightened, I hear a car pull off, screeching its tires. Fuck, they are getting away. I start to run toward the noise and then stop because I hear a faint moan in another room down the hall. I make a decision to check it out before I head to the back of the fort. I approach the room and I hesitate for a moment. My breathing picks up and I am actually scared at what

I might find behind the door. I then grow some balls and open the door with my gun pointed straight. I scan over the room and see Lily lying on a bed in the center of the room handcuffed to the post. She has no clothes on and she is barely moving. I run to her side and take the handcuffs off her.

"Oh my god. How could they do this to you? Oh, my god." I get her hands loose and they drop lifelessly on the bed. I then take the handcuffs off her feet. I immediately check her pulse to make sure she is still alive. "Please, baby, please be alive." It's weak, but she has a pulse. I cradle her in my arms and pull the blanket off the bed to wrap around her. I hear voices in the distance.

"Police, is anyone here?" an officer announces.

I yell out the door, "Down here, call EMS now. Please call EMS!" I choke. "Baby, please stay with me. Please stay with me." An officer enters the room and starts to panic. He is new and has no idea what to do.

"Get on the radio and request for EMS. We need everyone out looking for these shitheads. They have not gotten far." The officer just stands there and another enters the room. "Officer, look at me. I need you... Fuck it." I grab Lily in my arms and carry her to the SUV. I have the other officer get on the radio and call for backup and put up a perimeter.

"Don't let anyone in or out of this fort. I have to take Officer Matthews to the hospital."

"Shit, she is an officer?"

"Yes, so do your fucking job now." They all scramble around at my orders because they see how pissed off I am. This is fucking ridiculous.

I place Lily in the back seat and then I get into the driver seat. I drive off heading toward the hospital.

Lily is going in and out of consciousness and slurring her words.

"What did they do to you? I'm so sorry I wasn't there to protect you. I should have been there. I should have made you stay in my room. This is all my fault. I will finish this. Those fuckers are mine."

Riding lights and sirens, I make it to the hospital in ten minutes from Tybee Island. They knew I was coming because of dispatch. *Lily, hold on, my butterfly*. We are here. I pull up to the bay and jump out the SUV. I get Lily out of the back seat and run through the emergency room doors. I place her on the stretcher and the doctors and nurses take her. I hold on to her hand and one of the nurses puts their palm on my shoulder.

"You have to let her go so we can help her."

I am hesitant at first. I look into the nurse's eyes. "You have to save her. She is the love of my life." And for the first time in my life I shed tears I never thought I could for a woman.

"We will," the nurse promises, and she walks away with my butterfly.

Chapter 24

Lily

I hear voices in the distance, but I can't make them out. I try to open my eyes, but they won't open. I then take a deep breath and realize my throat hurts really bad. I need water. I try to reach for my throat, but nothing is moving.

I hear the voices again.

"She has been through a lot. Once she wakes up, she will need a lot of help and you will have to show a lot of patience. Do you understand?"

"Yes, I understand. I will not leave her side." I think that is Jason. My Jason is here. I still can't open my eyes.

"What are her injuries?"

"You're not family, so I shouldn't discuss her—"

"Please tell me, doc. She means everything to me. I love her."

Wait, Jason loves me?

"Okay but brace yourself. No person should have to go through what she went through and live to tell the story."

"I get it, doc."

"She has signs of being brutally raped. We found semen in her vagina and anus. She has three broken ribs, a broken nose, and a fractured jaw. Her arm was dislocated, and her hip suffered a lot of bruising. She will need lots of therapy, physically and mentally. It will be a tough road for her, but I am confident that if she takes it easy and follows our regimen, then she will do just fine."

Are they talking about me? Who could survive such trauma?

"Jesus, thanks, doc. I appreciate all your help. I've already called her sister and she is on her way."

Amelia, she's okay. Thank God. I try to reach for my throat again, but I can't.

I then feel someone squeeze my hand and whisper in my ear. "Baby, please come back to me. I love you and I can't live without you. Please, God, if you can, bring my love back. She means everything to me. I promise I will never put her in danger again. I promise to always protect her. If you give her back to me, I will give my life protecting hers. Please, God."

I squeeze his hand, letting him know he doesn't have to be scared. I am here and I love him too. I want to open my eyes so bad, but I can't.

"Doc, doc!" I hear Jason yell. "Lily squeezed my hand!" I hear the doctor walk back in and I try my very best to squeeze Jason's hand again as hard as I can.

"Doc, look. She is squeezing my hand. What does this mean? Is she waking up?"

Why are they talking like I am not right here? I hear you, Jason.

"Yes, she is trying to wake up, but the anesthesia is still wearing off. She should be waking up soon, but she will not stay awake for long. The medication will kick in. You do not want her being in the pain she will experience if the meds wear off completely."

I feel my eyes fluttering and for a minute, I don't know where I am. I try to talk, but my mouth is dry.

"Baby, don't try to talk. Just nod if you understand what I am saying."

I nod as hard as I can.

"That's it, baby. You are doing great."

I squeeze his hand, letting him know I can hear him. I then flutter my eyes open and I see the most beautiful eyes in the world. Green like a rain forest in the middle of spring.

"You have gorgeous eyes," I say. He starts to laugh and show me those perfect teeth.

"You have gorgeous eyes also, baby."

I wince because I feel a sharp pain in my side.

"Oh, sorry, baby. Try not to move. You have several injuries. The doc said you will be okay; you just have to take it easy."

I nod my head and start drifting back to sleep.

"I love you, baby."

I love you too.

Chapter 25

Jason

It's been three days and Lily still has been in and out of con-sciousness. The doctor said she has made progress, but I just don't understand why it is taking so long for her to recover. I understand what the doc is saying, but I selfishly want her back.

Amelia broke down when she finally saw her sister. She couldn't handle it, so I had an officer escort her and Dianella back to my place. I didn't want them at The Grind until we found those ass-holes who hurt my butterfly.

Just thinking about it makes my blood boil.

I spoke to Knight earlier. She has a good lead on the Page broth-ers, but she keeps coming up short. Captain Hill has put the whole force out there looking for these pricks. She believes that they are still in town because they haven't finished the job. She thinks they will try to come after Lily again. They probably will because they are sadistic assholes. And if they do, I will be ready for them.

Lily did kill one of them. That's my girl. She is bad ass. She always said she could take care of herself. And she was right. She managed to stay alive without my help. I am so proud of her.

Lily starts to move in her bed, and I am on my feet in seconds to be at her beck and call.

"Please, no." Fuck, she is having another nightmare; reliving the assault that was placed on her. I can't stand watching her reliving this shit. Please, God, stop torturing her. She doesn't deserve this. Please. I beg of you, please.

She opens her eyes wide, searching her surroundings. She then drifts her eyes to mine, and I witness the relief in her eyes. She reaches for my hand.

"Please don't leave me."

"I am never leaving your side again."

She closes her eyes and drifts back unconscious.

Chapter 26

Lily

I look around the room and I see concrete walls on all four sides. Candles flickering all around me and rose petals all over the bed. I see Jason with lust in his gaze. He wants me and only me. He starts to pull off his shirt and pants. He stalks toward me and pulls off my shirt and pants. He then guides me to the bed and pulls off my panties. I want him so bad; I feel my essence run down my leg. I am so wet for this man, this sex god. His abs are like slabs of bricks and his arms are the size of my thighs. I open to him and encourage him to give me all of him. His dick is so hard, so large, and so thick, I don't know how he will fit in me. He hovers over me and then bends down to kiss me. His kiss is so soft and purposeful. He continues the assault on my lips and then takes a much-needed breath. Once he pulls away, I open my eyes to look into his eye. I automatically tense with fear, anger, and rage. The eyes I see are not Jason's. These eyes belong to a hateful person. A person who hurt me. I begin to scream, and I can't hear my voice. I try to push him off, but my hands are bound with something. I look up and my hands are handcuffed to the bed. Shit, fuck. I have to get out of here. I twist and buck to get him off of me. I feel hands shaking me and I scream louder, but I can't hear myself. I hear someone else. *Jason, where are you. Please, Jason, come get me. Save me from this hell.*

"I'm right here, Lily. I'm not going anywhere." I open my eyes and I see Jason standing over me with fear and heartache in his eyes. "I'm here, Lily. I'm here. It's going to be okay." I reach up to hug him and I feel a sharp pain in my side.

"Shit, that hurts." I lie back down and take a deep breath.

"You just had a nightmare. Everything will be okay." I hear him, but I don't believe him. I keep reliving that horrible night and I can't stop thinking about it. So, I lie to him.

"I know." I try to sit up in the bed, but I have trouble moving.

"Here, let me help you." I let Jason help me sit up and even though it's painful, I feel a lot better when he helps me.

"Thank you."

"Anytime. I am always here to help you with anything. Are you thirsty or hungry?" Like being cued to act in a play, my stomach starts to growl. When was the last time I ate something?

"Yes, I am starving. How long have I've been here?"

"Four days."

"Seriously?"

"Yes, your body was subjected to a lot of trauma, so the doctor kept you in a medically induced coma to help with the swelling and recovery time."

"Did they say I would be okay."

"With a lot of physical and mental therapy and support, you should bounce right back, but it will take time."

Feeling relieved, I ask, "May I have some water?"

"Of course, baby." He reaches for the water on the table. "Here, drink through the straw. You can't move your jaw too much because of your injuries."

Curious about my injuries, I ask, "Can you tell me everything, please?" I see the dread in his eyes, and I know he doesn't want to relive that nightmare. "I need to know what happened to me. Please?"

With a long sigh, he begins to tell me the full report.

I still remember the devastation on Jason's face when he gave me my full report. Sitting in his room on the bed, I never really took a good look around. He really has a nice pad. Jason has been so good to me, feeding me, brushing my hair, and sitting with me so I won't be alone. Now that I am out of the hospital and under his roof, reality sets in. I am broken beyond repair. I try to put on a strong facade, but deep down, I don't want to be touched. I don't want anyone to see me at my weakest. If it wasn't for Amelia insisting that we stay with Jason, I would have gone home. It's not his job to take care of me. This is my fault and I should pay for what I did.

But, what exactly did I do? Adam kept saying this was all my fault. Maybe it is. Maybe I should have been in that car with my sister and parents as well. Maybe I was meant to die with them.

I don't know what to do. "Fuck this, I hate this." I throw the pillow as hard as I can, and it knocks over a vase. Shit.

Jason runs into the room. "Are you okay?"

Feeling overwhelmed, I yell at him. "Stop asking me that. I will never be okay. This is all my fault." Tears are running down my face and I can't stop them; they have a mind of their own, creating two streams on my cheeks and dropping down on my clothes.

"Baby, please. This is not your fault."

"Yes, it is. Just leave me alone." I pull the covers over my head and turn my back on him. For a while there's dead silence and then I hear the door close. I shouldn't be mad at him, but I am. He was too late in saving me. He let those assholes rape me. I hate him for not protecting me.

Fuck, I am so confused. I just want all of this to go away. I can't take it anymore.

I must have drifted away because I feel a light touch on my shoulder. I jump up. "Shit, that hurt."

"Easy, Lily, It's just me." I look up and see worry in my sister's eyes. I know that look so well. She always had it when we first lost our parents. She always wanted me to cuddle with her and rock her to sleep. But I just can't right now. I just want to be left alone.

"What do you want?" I spit at her with frustration and disdain.

"I wanted to see how you were holding up. You are starting to look a lot better. The bruising has gone down. But we are worried about you. You are not eating properly; you won't get out of bed, and you are treating everyone like shit. We are just trying to help."

"Well, I didn't ask for your help, so just leave."

"I'm not going anywhere. You are my sister and just like you were there for me, I will be here for you. I don't give a damn how much you try to push me away. And you need to stop being so mean to Jason. That man right there loves you and if you can't see that, then you don't deserve him. He has done everything for you. He has taken care of me and Dianella and made sure we were safe. So, get off your ass and get your shit together. I will not allow you to go another day treating people like shit. Do I make myself clear?"

Holy shit, the roles have changed. She is now my keeper and I am the child. How the fuck did that happen.

"Answer me now?"

"Okay, I will try to do better." Flabbergasted I just sit there for more instructions.

"It's time to take a shower. It's been a week and you smell like shit. How the fuck does Jason stand to be around you?"

For the first time in a long time I laugh. "Shit, that hurts. But I needed it." I start to get out of the bed, but I need help. My ribs still hurt, my ankles are killing me, and my face feel like shit. "Can you help me please?" I say, pleading with my eyes.

"No, Jason will help you, and you will be okay with it. I have to go to school. I have a class." She looks at me and gives me a hug. "I love you, sis, but you have to let him help you. You will regret it later if you don't."

"I don't want him to see me like this. I don't want him to see me naked. I am scared."

"I understand, but someone has to help you and I can't. I've already missed so much schoolwork. I have to catch up if I want to graduate on time."

"I get it." Reluctantly, I ask, "Can you ask him to come here?"

"Yes; and apologize to him. He doesn't deserve to be treated this way."

"Fine."

She gives me a kiss on my forehead and then walks out. I don't know if I can do this.

A moment later, Jason walks into the room. He seems taller than the last time I saw him. His posture is straight with confidence. I see a little hesitation in his eyes. Probably because I've treated him like shit for the past two weeks. He stands watching me, waiting for me to say something.

"I want to apologize for treating you like shit lately. You don't deserve it and I'm sorry."

"It's okay, baby. You can't get rid of me even if you tried."

I try to stand up on my own but fall back down.

"Shit, I hate this. I hate being so weak."

"You will get your strength back; you just have to take your time and rely on me for strength for now. Are you okay with that?"

Am I okay with that? I am so frustrated about this whole thing. Ignoring his question, I say, "Can you help me to the bathroom? Apparently, I smell like shit."

He drops the questioning and helps me to the bathroom. "Do you need help taking your clothes off?"

"No, I'm okay, but can you turn the shower on and get me a washcloth and towel?"

"Absolutely." He walks out and a few minutes later he come back with a washcloth and a towel. He turns on the water and walks toward the door.

"If you need anything else, I will be sitting in the bedroom."

"Thank you."

He stares at me with sincerity in his eyes for a little while and then walks out the bathroom, closing the door behind him.

I take off my shirt first. It hurts so bad, but I am so stubborn I endure the pain. I take the shirt over my head slowly and proceed to my pants. I pull my bra straps down one by one and turn it so I can unfasten the snaps. I then take my panties off slowly, letting them fall to the floor. I then move to the mirror because this is the first time I've looked at myself in the mirror. I am horrified at what I see. There are black and blue bruises all over my stomach, legs, and arms. My face looks like I went in the ring with a boxing champ. I have never seen anything like it. I sink to the floor and I just start crying. Crying a hard, loud, ugly cry. I cry because I am mad. I cry because I am enraged. I cry because I am losing all hope in myself. I am ugly now. No one will want me now, not even Jason. I can't stop crying. I hear a knock on the door, and I continue to cry.

"Lily, is everything okay?" I continue to cry. He walks in cautiously and finds me on the floor. He rushes over to me and asks again if I am okay. I continue to cry. I can't stop. I cry for the time I was strong. I cry for the time I was scared. I cry for all the times I had to fight for myself.

Jason picks me off the floor and puts me in the shower. He gets in with me even though he is fully clothed. I don't want him to see me like this, but I can't stop crying. He gets a loofa and fills it with bodywash. He then starts to wash my back for me because I am incapable of doing it myself. He washes my arms and my legs. I continue to cry in his arms. He doesn't touch me anywhere else and lets the water run over both of us. He holds me until I stop crying. I just lie in his arms and I can't move. He strokes my hair gently to comfort me. He doesn't say anything; he just holds me. Once the water starts to get lukewarm, he turns it off. He picks me up and grabs a towel. He dries me off and then picks me up again and takes me to bed. He puts one of his t-shirts on me and then tucks me in bed. He takes his clothes off and puts on his boxers and a t-shirt. He then gets in bed with me and holds me in his arms until I fall asleep. He doesn't say one word. He's just there for me. And that is the first time after I was raped that I truly felt comforted.

Chapter 27

Jason

I'm sitting on the balcony of my home with Ryan, my best friend. He called me earlier wanting me to go out, but I turned him down. I need to stay home to watch over Lily. She has calmed down a lot since the other night when she had a mental breakdown. The psychologist told me if that ever happened, just be there for her and let her know you care without saying a word. She doesn't want to hear your sympathies. She just wants to be understood. So, I did exactly what the doctor said, and it seemed to work.

We both have Tennessee mules in our hand as we listen to the hustle and bustle of downtown Savannah.

"You really need to find these assholes. I don't know how you do it."

Oh, I know how. I love this girl with all my heart, and I am never letting her get away from me again. I am even overprotective of her sister as well. She is my family also and I will take care of all of them. I make her and Dianella send me a text every hour, no exceptions. If they want to go to school, then they will abide by my rules. I gave Amelia a tracking bracelet as well. That bracelet saved Lily's life. I am so glad I gave it to her.

"I do it because I love her."

"Wow, I never ever heard you say that about anyone."

"That's because she's the one. She is the love of my life and I will do anything for her. I will kill for her. I will die for her."

"You're serious." He sounds surprised by my confession.

"Yes, I am dead serious. Once this mess is over with and she is back on her feet, I am going to ask her to marry me."

"Holy shit. This is serious." He takes a huge chug of his drink. "Good for you. You know I'm your best man?" he says with a smirk on his face.

"I wouldn't have it any other way." My phone pings. It's Knight.

> *I'm on my way to your place.*
> *I have something to show you.*

> *Okay, swing through.*
> *Ryan is here too.*

I see the three little dots like she is going to respond, but then they go away.

"Hey, Knight is on her way." I watch his behavior and he physically tenses up. "Is everything okay with you and Knight?"

He takes another drink. "Yeah, everything is good. Why do you ask?"

"Because I know you better than you know yourself. And I know when something is up."

"We just haven't seen much of each other lately."

Shit, that's my fault. "Yeah, we have been very busy with the case. It gets like that sometimes, you know?"

"I get it. I just wish she would call and say hi at least."

"Do you call her?" Silence gives me everything I need to know. "Knight is much like Lily; they have both been through some horrible shit. You might want to reach out and just say hey or what's up. It will go a long way."

"Thanks for the advice." The doorbell rings and he almost drops his glass on the balcony.

"Easy, it's just Knight." He flashes me a fuck-you look and I throw him a smirk. I then walk toward the door and let her in. "Hey, Knight, how's it going?"

"I've seen better days. I wish this shit was over with."

"Ain't that the truth."

"How is she doing?"

"As good as expected. She is resting now. We were sitting on the balcony. You want a drink?"

"No, I am on call. Can't drink tonight."

"Okay, what's up? What did you want to show me?"

"There was a DVD that was sent to the office. It's very disturbing, but I think you should watch it. I wouldn't ask if it wasn't important." I see the fear in her eyes and also a hint of being horrified. "It is very graphic and definitely do not let Lily see this."

"You are scaring me. What's on the DVD?"

"Everything."

I am sitting in my study and I get ready to pop the DVD into my flat screen TV on the wall. My study is soundproof, so Lily won't hear anything. I hesitate a little before I push play.

"Here goes nothing."

It starts off by showing the triplets, Adam, Andrew, and Anthony, goofing around. Then it switches to a girl handcuffed to a bed and one of the triplets fucking her. I look closely and it's one of the victims. It looks like the first victim. It then switches to another victim being raped by one of the triplets. It switches three more times before it switches to one female in particular. She is handcuffed to the bed with no clothes on. It looks like she is passed out. I recognize the girl because of her hair. It's Lily. She starts to come to and one of the triplets starts talking to her. He tells her why she is there and then one of the triplets forces one of the brothers to fuck her. I feel tears burning the back of my eyes and I am infuriated at this point. I can't turn it off. I keep watching. He gets on top of her and he is fucking my butterfly over and over again. She is begging him to stop, but he doesn't. She is no longer scared. It looks like she forces herself to think about everything else but what is happening to her. He then finishes. And because she doesn't seem pleased, he beats her repeatedly. She doesn't give him the satisfaction of making a sound. The other brother then pulls him off and he starts to fuck her, but he is interrupted by something. He is interrupted by me.

I search for the trash can and I hurl everything I've ever eaten up. I knock everything off my desk. I throw shit everywhere.

Knight and Ryan walk in and I damn near knock them to the ground. Ryan grabs me by the shoulders and wraps his arms around me to force me to stop.

"It's okay, bro. It's okay."

"It's not okay. She…she…she." I can't speak; I can't breathe. "I should have gotten there sooner. They raped my butterfly, and I didn't protect her. They beat her and she didn't say a fucking word. She was so fearless, and I couldn't protect her." I drop to my knees and rock back and forth, crying my eyes out. I can't believe they did that to her. Why her? Why not me?" I knew she went through hell, but never could I ever imagine this.

"This is not your fault. It's none of your faults. These people are sick and twisted. There is no way we could have known this was going to happen."

"She knew. She broke the profile down to the very description of their obsession. She knew. Fuck, and I let her stay in that room by herself anyway. I did this to her."

"Stop it right now." I look up at Lily standing in the doorway. "This is not your fault. If anyone should be to blame, it should be me. I made a decision because I was insecure. That is not your fault. You were respecting my wishes. What those sick fucks did to me is not our fault. They had this planned down to the very second. If it wasn't for this," she raises her wrist up with the tracking device on it, "I wouldn't be alive today. You saved me." She walks toward me and places both palms on my cheeks. "You are a good man. You would have never deliberately put me in danger. None of us knew that Andrew was setting us up. We could not have predicted that. He planned all of this. He is the mastermind and his brothers are the undertakers. He got what he wanted, but he didn't take my soul. He didn't take my pride. He didn't take my love. Do you understand me?"

I nod my head because I am too weak to speak.

She pulls me into her arms and winces a little because she is still in pain, but she won't let me hold her. She holds me. Knight and Ryan walk out and give us privacy.

"I'm in love with you, Lily. I've been in love with you for a long time, I just never said anything. It scares the hell out of me and I don't know what to do, but I know that I am wholeheartedly, undeniably in love with you. I know we work together, and I don't want things to be—"

She places a finger on my lips. "I'm in love with you also, Jason. I've loved you since the first night we were together. To be honest, I hated you at first, but then I realized you are my everything. I find myself opening up to you in a way I could never do with anyone else. You see me and only me. You are there for me through all my crazy ups and downs and you never judged me; you never gave up on me even when I tried to push you away. I love you too."

I then smash my lips to hers and devour her like it is the first time I've ever kissed her, and she opens up to me willingly. She gives me all of her and I give her all of me in this very moment. I know she is not ready to make love, but this will definitely do.

Chapter 28

Lily

Several weeks have passed by and we still haven't found Page. I've gotten my strength back and I feel 90 percent better than I did weeks ago. I return to work today even though Jason was furious about it. He made me keep a bodyguard at all times if I wanted to head back. I finally gave in and allowed him to hire a bodyguard. What would a bodyguard do that I couldn't do?

I get dressed and head into work. Getting dressed doesn't hurt as much as it did weeks ago. Jason refused to let me see the video that was sent to the office. He said he compromised with the bodyguard, but he put his foot down with the video. I tried to explain to him that I needed to watch it to develop some more leads. But he would not budge. So, I just have to go by memory. He is due to come to work later today as well, but he has to stop by The Grind to check on some inventory. Knight gave me all new access cards because Page might have access to the office.

She wanted to take all precautious before I returned back to work. She is such a good friend.

I enter the building with my bodyguard on my ass.

"Welcome back, Detective Matthews!" several people yell the moment I walk into the office. The whole squad is there, including Jason. How the hell did they pull this off without me noticing?

Jason gives me a knowing smirk. Hold up, wait a minute.

"Detective Matthews?" I ask, astonished.

"Yes, baby. You are officially a detective."

"Wow, I don't know what to say."

"Say thank you and I love you."

"Yes, right, thank you and I think I love you." I smack him on the arm playfully and he grabs me and gives me a kiss.

"Wait, not at work. We talked about this."

"Yes, we did. And I don't give a damn who sees me kiss my girl. You are mine." He grabs me again, bends me backward, and kisses me fully and with absolute passion. I still haven't had the courage to have sex with him yet. I still have nightmares, but not as much as...

He pulls away and everyone yelps and roars. "Now that's how you kiss your woman."

I've grown fond of these guys and wouldn't trade them for the world. Kim hands me a cup of coffee and my favorite cheese Danish from The Grind.

"Now I see what you two have been up to. I should have known it was odd for you not to escort me to work on my first day back." Jason and Kim flash me smiles and give each other high-fives.

"We finally were able to surprise you without you finding out. It's about time," Kim says.

I sit down in the chair because I am a little exhausted from standing up. This excitement has gotten to me a little. "Baby, are you okay? Do you need anything?"

"No, I'm fine. Just need to sit down for a little." Part of the agreement with Jason was I would stay in the office and do desk work until I was at 100 percent. I understand why, now.

He pats me on the shoulder and gives me a kiss on the forehead. I have to get used to that at work. I never wanted my personal life to interfere with my professional life, and now both worlds have collided. Literally. He walks away and heads over to the captain. They both enter the captain's office.

"You know, he really does care about you. I've never seen him with anyone like I've seen him with you," Kim says.

"Yes, I am starting to realize that. I just always wanted my private life separate from my work life. You know?"

"Yeah, I get it. I am the same way, but things tend to find their way together anyway."

"You got that right."

"Oh, I almost forgot, you have your own office with a great view of the city. It's between my office and Hall's office."

"Wow, I get my own office too?"

"Yes, of course. We all do."

I didn't think about that either. "Do you think it would be okay to share an office with you? I really don't want to be alone right now."

"Say no more. I will have some of the guys move your stuff into my office. It's big enough for an army anyway."

I smile at Kim, letting her know that I appreciate her more than she knows. I am going to have to do something for her soon. She has really been there for me.

"Hey, you three? Help me move Matthews' desk and stuff in my office. We are roomies now." She flashes me a smile. "I got this." She stands up and heads to her office to get it ready. I sit and watch her go.

I thought I would be nervous coming back to work because all of these guys saw me at my worst, but they have shown me nothing but love. They all seem to genuinely have my back and I couldn't be more thankful.

"Okay, Lily, we are done," Kim announces. "You can now see your quarters." I laugh a little too hard and grab my side. "Don't laugh too hard; you're bound to pull a muscle."

And I belly over and start laughing even more, not caring about the pain. I so needed this. I get up and head to my new quarters. "Wow, I am impressed."

"Hall said nothing but the best for his girl."

I blush because no one has ever showed that much affection toward me in my life. Well, except for my dad, but that doesn't count.

"Thank you both."

"You're welcome, Butterfly." I turn around and see the most handsome guy standing in the doorway. He is sexier than I ever realized, with strong arms, confident posture, and a physique that puts Tom Cruise to shame. This fine specimen is all mine. I can't keep my eyes from eye-fucking him. I want to have him, but I am too afraid right now. The therapist said if I am not ready, then don't force it. But damn.

"Knight and I have to head out to work on a case. Are you good here?"

"Where are y'all going?"

"We need to do some follow-ups. If you need anything, call me. And of course, you have Jacob here to get you whatever you want."

Shit, I forgot just that quick about my bodyguard, who is hovering outside the door. "You know I don't need a bodyguard. It's like Fort Knox in here."

"Yes, I know, but I will not take any chances."

I lower my gaze because I feel so defeated.

"It's okay. You will be fine, Lily," Kim says.

I nod my head and they both walk away.

I'm sitting at my new desk and I actually feel comfortable. The captain has assigned me small cases to work at the office and do callbacks for the guys. I have turned into a glorified secretary. But if I want to come to work, then I have to do what they ask. I am tired of sitting around in the house. Don't get me wrong, I love being at Jason's, but I need to do something. Now that I think about it, I haven't been home in weeks. Maybe I should head over there sometime to grab a few things and to tidy up the place.

I begin to make my first round of callbacks. After about three hours, I start looking at my first case. It's about a missing girl in her twenties. Her parents haven't seen her in five days. According to the police report, she is in school working on her bachelor's degrees in Business Administration. She attends dance classes at night and that is the last time anyone has seen her. I pick up the phone and call her mother, Mrs. Johnson.

"Hello?"

"Hi, may I speak to Mrs. Johnson?"

"Speaking."

"Hi, I am Detective Matthews with Savannah Police Department. The reason for my call—"

"I know the reason. Have you found my daughter?"

"No ma'am, not yet. But I have a few questions."

"I've already answered several questions of the police officer; what else do you need?"

"Is your daughter adopted?"

"What does her adoption have to do with her being missing?"

My heart starts to accelerate. "It has a lot to do with it. Did she ever live at Greenbriar?"

"Yes, she did. She was there for most of her childhood before she came to live with me. I adopted her ten years ago."

"Thank you, Mrs. Johnson. I think I have a lead, but I am not sure yet. I will call you if I find anything."

"Oh, thank God. Please call me day or night. I haven't been able to sleep since she went missing."

"Of course." We hang up and then I call Jason immediately. He picks up on the first ring.

"Butterfly?"

"Yes, it's me. I think there is another missing girl."

"How do you know this?"

"It's one of the cases captain assigned me."

He sounds frustrated. "What are the details?"

"Well, the girl is in her twenties. She attends Georgia college and she was adopted from Greenbriar ten years ago."

"Shit, they are back."

"What do you mean?"

"Fuck, I said too much. Send me the case and Knight and I will take it from here."

"No, I want to help."

"Absolutely not." I can hear the sternness in his voice. "Lily, I don't want you anywhere near this case. Do I make myself clear?" I'm quiet because I don't know what to say. "Answer me."

"Fine, but you can't keep this from me forever."

"You bet your ass I can." He hangs up the phone. I hear Jacob talking to someone on the phone.

"Yes sir, she will not leave my sight."

Asshole. I need to get out of here without Jacob knowing. But how will I do that?

I put the folder in my purse.

"Hey Jacob, I have to head to the bathroom and then I want to leave to get something to eat."

"Okay, Ms. Matthews."

"You can call me Lily."

"Yes ma'am."

I head to the bathroom and lock the door behind me. I need to find a way out of here. I look around and find a window. I head toward the window and notice bars blocking entry into the bathroom. Shoot. *Think, Lily, think.* I can't leave this office without someone noticing. Oh, well. I need to just let it go. But that's not my nature. I need to be able to catch these assholes. I am the only one they want, not these other girls. And then it dawns on me. I am the answer.

Chapter 29

Jason

Knight and I have been working around the clock trying to find these guys. We turned over every rock we could find, but still no sign.

Now Lily calls with information about a possible abduction of another girl. They are trying to fish Lily out so they can have the ultimate prize.

"We have one more place to check and then we can head back to the office," says Knight.

"Okay, let's go after that. I haven't left Lily alone this long since—"

"How is she doing?"

"As well as expected. She is still having nightmares, but not as often."

"That's progress, right?"

"Yes, the doctor said it's great progress. I just wish I could take away her nightmares."

"It will take time. Don't rush it. I just wish someone cared about me as much as you care about Lily."

"What do you mean? You have Ryan."

"We both are very busy and after Lily being kidnapped, he became possessive and didn't want me working on the case anymore. This is my life; I will never give it up. He needs to be strong enough to accept that, and I really don't do possessive. I think you know that about me."

Yes, I know too well how she was when her last boyfriend tried to kill her.

"I think you should give him a chance. He really isn't like that. He is a good guy."

"Well, I am tired of fighting for a man. It's time for them to fight for me."

I get her point. It should be a give and take, not one-sided. I am beginning to understand that more now than I ever had before.

We pull up to an abandoned house on West 31st Street. We ran a trace on all the utilities and mail that Andrew, Adam, and Anthony were receiving. We also ran a background on their sister, Abby, just to cover our bases. It turns out that they all used to live at this house but were removed when their mother died.

This was the last address we had to check on. All the other address came up empty.

Knight pulls into the lane so we won't be so obvious to the neighbors. We get out of the car and approach the back door. Knight tries the lock and to our avail, it is open.

We enter with our weapons drawn. Once I enter the kitchen area, I smell a faint trace of perfume. I've smelled that perfume before. We continue toward the living room, where there is old furniture covered with sheets. There are old photos on the wall; photos of the triplets and Abby. They seem happy in the photos but looks can be deceiving. We continue toward the staircase. There is a basement and a second floor. We decide to head toward the basement.

Knight opens the door and starts to go down first. I pull her and signal for her to get behind me. I am not letting anything happen to her. Reluctantly, she does what I ask. I walk down the stairs, and that smell gets stronger. It smells just like Lily.

My heart starts to race, and I feel like I am back at the fort finding her handcuffed to a bed naked. I shake that thought out of my head and continue on with Knight on my heel.

With my flashlight out, I scan the area. I see several plants all over the place. The same plants that were in the squares. I then see camera equipment like a photoshoot is about to happen. I then see an old bed in the middle of the room with lily pad-like plants surrounding the bed. There are candles surrounding the bed as well.

"This is where they take the girls to do the photoshoot and then kill them. Then they take the girls to one of squares to dump the body," Knight says.

"Knight, we found it. You found it," I say with excitement in my voice.

"Now what?"

"We need to set up surveillance and wait for their return."

Chapter 30

Lily

I send Anthony a text message.

> *Hi asshole.*

Now I just wait for his response. I know he can't resist me. He will answer and that is when I hook him.

> *Hi, Lily. It's so nice of you to send me a message? How are you?*

> *I am perfectly fine.*

> Glad to hear. I was worried about you.

Drop the act. You don't give a damn about me.

> I beg to differ. I love you, Lily.

I want this to stop.

> The only way this stops is if you offer yourself to us in exchange of a poor soul.

Fine, when and where?

> 404 West 31st Street, now.

On my way.

This will finally end; whether I live or die, this will finally be over. No more innocent girls will have to die because of me. I send Jason a text.

I love you.

I head to the house with Jacob, and I change into black tights and a neon pink tank top with matching sneakers. I put my hair in a high ponytail. I have a hidden compartment in my bra and tights. I put razor blades in both compartments, and I position one in my hair. If they find the first two, I can have a backup. I keep the bracelet that Jason gave me on my left wrist so he can find me if I die.

Now I need to get rid of Jacob. I grab my taser and walk toward him in the kitchen. I put it in his side and turn it on. He hits the floor immediately. I then handcuff him to the door handle of the fridge. I grab his phone and toss it in the trash. I just need enough time to get downstairs to my car.

I grab my keys and phone and hit the door before Jacob realizes what I did to him. I make it to my car with a sigh of relief. First part down, now for the grand finale.

I pull out of the garage and head south on Whittaker Street toward 404 West 31st Street. I pull up to the front of the house. There is only street parking, so I leave the car on the curb. I then walk up to the porch and my heart starts to beat rapidly. I don't know how I am going to do this, but I have to try. I place my hand on the door handle and I turn it. The door opens and I walk in.

There are candles everywhere and the smell of my perfume. It brings me back to the night they raped and beat me, and my heart feels like it's about to burst out of my chest. But I take a deep breath and continue to walk forward. I follow the trail of the candles to the basement.

Once I reach the bottom, I find a young girl tied up on the floor. She looks about the same age as my sister. She looks at me with absolute fear in her eyes. I come up to her and she tries to get away from me. I stop and put my hands up.

"I am not here to hurt you. I am a police officer and I want to help." She lights up with hope in her eyes and I pull the gag out of her mouth.

"Please help me. They are going to kill me."

"No, they won't. They have to go through me first." I begin to untie her.

"Well, well, well. If it isn't Lily Matthews to the rescue."

I place my body in front of the girl to protect her. "Let her go. I am who you want."

"I told you I would make a trade. I always keep my promises. A body for a body."

I turn to look at the girl. "Once I tell you to run, you run as fast as you can and never look back. Do you understand me?"

She nods her head.

"Lily, you are more beautiful than I remember, and you heal very well."

"Cut the shit. Where is your brother?"

"Oh, he is enjoying himself right now. We had a two-for-one deal. These young idiots make it too easy these days."

Shit, there's another girl. "Let both of them go and you can do whatever you want with me."

"Intriguing offer. I will have to discuss with my brother."

"What, you can't make decisions for him?"

"We share everything if you haven't realized."

I hear the girl sobbing behind me and praying.

"Fine, call your pussy ass brother down here. I am ready to get this over with."

"Feisty, aren't we? I love it." He claps his hands together like he is enjoying my presentation. He pulls his phone out and calls his brother. "Anthony, hurry the fuck up and bring the bitch with you." He hangs up the phone and then stares at me like he is fantasizing about me naked. He is more creepy than his brother. How are people like this created?

I hear footsteps and cries coming from upstairs.

"Perfect, now we can have a party."

"Let them go and I will give you anything you want."

"Don't push me, bitch, or I will fucking kill all three of you and fuck your dying corpses."

Not wanting to push him, I close my mouth.

Anthony and the other girl finally make it downstairs. He must have beat her because she is now unconscious.

"What did you do to her?" I scream at him.

"Nothing, the bitch deserved it," says Anthony.

"Lily here has made an offer I don't want to refuse."

"Yeah, what's that?"

"Well, she will give us whatever we want if we let these poor souls go. What do you think about that offer?" He taps his finger on his chin like he really is thinking about my offer.

"I think we can accept that. I have so many things I want to do with her."

I grunt a little because I feel like throwing up, but I force it down. I will not show these assholes fear.

Anthony kicks the girl on the floor in the stomach. "Get up, bitch." She doubles down in pain and cradle herself like a baby. She has no clothes on and there is blood everywhere. She will need a doctor immediately.

The girl finally gets up slowly. "Run," Andrew whispers. The girl looks terrified, almost like this is a trick, but she turns anyway and takes off running upstairs.

They then turn their focus on the girl behind me. "Get up now." She gets up slowly as well. "Run, now." She looks back at me, mouths "thank you," and takes off running.

I pray they find help immediately because I am going to need it.

Now, they both turn to me like vultures circling their prey.

"Andrew, you go first since I went first the last time." A big smile runs across his face and it's the creepiest thing I've ever seen. But I have to take control of the situation.

"Why don't you both take me together? You say you share everything, why not share me together?"

"Now, that is something to experience. We haven't had a threesome in a long time, brother."

"Yes, you're right."

"Strip your clothes off and lay on the bed."

I start to take my clothes off piece by piece. I want to turn these assholes on so I can control this. Once I drop all of my garments on the ground, they watch me with intense and heavy eyes. I can see them get hard for me and I encourage them to get harder.

I lie on the bed and I start playing with my pussy while they watch.

"Fuck, that is sexy as fuck." They both start to take off their clothes. "Andrew, you fuck her pussy and I will fuck her mouth."

Andrew gets on top of me and inserts his dick inside of me. "Fuck, you are so wet." He then starts to pump inside of me.

Anthony stands over me and grabs my head and turns my mouth toward his dick. I open wide for him and he puts it in. He starts to moan as well. I suck and I suck and watch his head lean backward. Andrew is lost in my pussy, and has no idea what I am about to do. Once I think they are about to come, I pull the blade out of my hair and slice underneath Anthony's balls first. I then take the blade and slice Andrew's neck.

Blood squirts everywhere. Andrew grabs his neck to try to stop the bleeding, but I damn near cut through his spine. I push Andrew off of me and let him drown in his own blood. I then bite down on Anthony's dick and rip a chunk off. He doubles down and screams.

"Fuck." I take the blade and slice his throat as well. I get on top of him and stab over and over with the blade until someone grabs my hands.

I swing the blade at the person, and they jump back. I can't see who it is because I have blood in my eyes.

"Lily, it's me. Lily, it's Jason."

Once I recognize the voice, I drop the blade and fall to my knees. I take a much-needed breath and I scream at the top of my lungs.

It's over. It's finally over and I am still alive.

Chapter 31

Jason

Seeing Lily once again naked with blood all over her scared the hell out of me. Once again, I thought I lost her. She will never understand the pain I felt thinking she was dead once again. When those girls came running out of that house, I knew something was terribly wrong. They said that a woman had saved them, and I just knew Lily went after those pricks when I told her not to.

I am so fucking pissed right now; I don't know what to do. I covered her up once again and took her to the hospital. This time they released her the same day. I then took her home. I feel so betrayed right now; more hurt than anything. Everything I have done for her and she just slaps me in the face and puts her life in danger anyway. I can't take it anymore. I'm about to combust with rage and fury.

We walk in the house and she heads for the bedroom. She hasn't said a word to me, and I haven't to her. I stalk behind her.

"I want you to get your shit and get the fuck out of my house."

She turns around and looks at me with hurt, sadness, and frustration in her eyes. "What did you say?"

"I said, get your shit and get the fuck out."

"Why are you saying those things?"

"You deliberately put yourself in danger once again without thinking what it could do to me or your sister. I can't keep going through this with you."

"Going through what?"

"You have no respect for me or anyone else. You only think about yourself. You are a selfish bitch and I want you gone."

She no longer looks at me with hurt; she now has rage in her eyes.

"Fuck you, Jason. You know what, you have no idea what it feels like being stalked, tortured, raped, and beaten. You don't know how it feels to constantly look over your shoulder to see when your time is up. So, don't give me that shit that I am selfish. I saved two girls who were about to have the same fate as all the other girls because of me. I gave myself to help them and anyone else who would have been tortured. I sacrificed myself for everyone. So, fuck you." I bow my head and feel like a complete asshole.

"I...I..."

She puts her hand up.

"Don't. I am leaving. I don't want to put you through any more heartache than I already have. Bye, Jason. I will have Amelia get my shit. Or you can burn it for all I care. I don't want any of it." She then turns around and walks out of my room.

Chapter 32

Lily

I've been lying in my bed for a week, crying my heart out. I lost everything. I lost my will to live, I lost my parents, I lost Jason, and now I have nothing.

I keep replaying the breakup in my head and every time, it gets worse and worse. I love Jason with all my heart, and I knew he would be mad, but not that mad. How could he say those hurtful things to me. Everything I do, I do it for everyone else. I am not selfish. I may be high-strung, independent, and confident, but I am not selfish. Fuck him for saying that I am.

Shit, I am on an emotional roller coaster and I don't know how to jump off.

I hear footsteps enter my room and I pull my gun out and point it.

"Don't shoot, it's me, Lily. Your only sister."

"Shit, what did I tell you about sneaking up on me?"

"Well, you aren't answering your phone for anyone. So, they are calling me. You won't even answer the phone for me, so I knew something was up. What's going on? Why is Jason calling me looking for you?"

"Fuck Jason; he dumped me. He called me a selfish bitch. So, he can just go to hell."

"I know you don't mean that, so drop the act. Have you forgotten who you're talking to?"

I look at her and start to cry again. "It hurts so much, Amelia. I just want it to stop."

"I know it does, but you can't stay in this bed forever. You can't allow those assholes to win. Not now; not ever."

"I know, but what am I supposed to do?"

"Well, for starters you can go take a shower. You smell like shit. Then you can go get your man back."

"I don't think I can do that."

"Yes, you can. Now get your ass up and get dressed. I brought you some food. I will be waiting in the kitchen."

She walks out of my room and I manage to roll out of bed. She is right, I need to get my shit together. I head to the bathroom and I feel like I need to vomit. I run to the toilet and let all my insides out. How the hell am I throwing up and I haven't eaten anything in a week?

It's probably just anxiety. I turn on the shower, take my clothes off, and step in. I let the hot water run over me and it feels like heaven. I stand there for about ten minutes before I actually start to bathe. I lather the bodywash in my loofa and scrub my body clean. I then take the washcloth and clean my face. I step out of the shower and dry off. I put clean clothes on and head to the kitchen.

Amelia is sitting at the counter and has a plate ready for me. My stomach starts to growl.

"See, you are hungry."

"Oh my gosh, this food tastes so good. I am so hungry." After a few more bites, I feel like I have to throw up again. I grab my stomach and run for the bathroom. I empty out my stomach again. I clean my face off and head back to the kitchen.

"Are you okay?"

"I don't know. That is the second time I've thrown up today."

"Maybe you need to go see a doctor. You have been under a ton of stress and your body is probably fighting off a virus."

"I hope you are right."

"Unless you are pregnant. That can't be possible, can it?"

My skin turns ice cold and my hands begin to shake.

"I...I can't be. Can I?"

"Oh, Lily, please tell me you took the morning after pill."

"I'm not sure. I was in and out of consciousness the first time I was—"

"When was the last time you had a period?"

Now that I think about it, I can't remember when.

"I think two months ago."

"Shit, I am making you an appointment first thing in the morning."

"What if—?"

"No, we will not claim that. Do I make myself clear?"

"Amelia, I'm scared."

"I know, honey. No matter what happens tomorrow, I will be here for you."

Amelia and I arrive at the doctor's office first thing in the morning. I am in a blue gown and awaiting my results. I am a total wreck. The only reason I haven't fallen apart yet is because my sister is here holding my hand.

"What if I am? What am I going to do?" I'm asking more so to myself than to Amelia. But she answers anyway.

"We will take care of her, nourish her, and give her all the love she deserves. Plus, I want to be an auntie."

I spread a slight smile on my lips and for the first time I realize that this could be a good thing. Not a bad one.

The doctor walks in twenty minutes later.

"Congratulation, you will be a mommy."

At that very moment tears start to fall down my cheek. I feel happiness and sadness. My feelings and emotions are everywhere. Amelia squeezes my hand to encourage me to continue to listen.

"You are about nine weeks pregnant. Would you like to take a look at your baby?" I try to do the math in my head. Nine weeks ago, I was making love to Jason without a condom for the first time.

"Dr. Lewis, I was on the shot. How is this possible?"

"Well, you never came in to get your shots updated. I left you several messages, but you never responded back."

Shit, I remember seeing the messages, but I was so busy with the case, I never thought twice about it.

"Dr. Lewis, I was in a situation about a month ago. Could that hurt the baby?" I know she read my chart and realized that I was beaten and brutally raped.

"The baby should be fine, but we will take a look to make sure. Lily, I know you have concerns, but this is a blessing for you. You always have options as well. But you must think about all your options before you make a decision, okay?"

"Yes ma'am, I understand."

Amelia squeezes my hand, once more letting me know she is here with me. I am not alone in this.

The doctor sets up the sonogram so I can meet my son or daughter. She lifts my gown up and squeezes gel on my stomach. Surprisingly, the gel is warm. She then places the sonogram on my stomach.

We start hearing bubbly noises. "What is that?"

"It's the baby's heartbeat."

Wow, my baby has a strong heartbeat. But then I notice some other noise.

"Is that my heartbeat also that I hear?" I look at the screen and I am amazed at what I see.

"Actually, Lily, there are two more heartbeats."

"What do you mean?"

"Lily, you are having triplets."

Chapter 33

Jason

It's a breezy and chilly night, but I don't care. I can't feel any-thing anyway. Sitting on my balcony, I take a drink of my Tennessee mule and the liquid burn down my throat. I never felt hopeless or pain like this before. It's been two weeks since I have seen Lily. I thought I would see her at the office, but she refuses to come to work. She requested time off to recover from her recent torture.

I feel like shit right now and I can't stop the feeling. I go to work and then I come home and pass out from drinking too much. My liver is probably shot because of all the whiskey I have in-gested over the past two weeks.

I miss Lily's beautiful smile and lovable demeanor. I really hurt her and now she wants nothing to do with me. She has ignored all of my text messages and phone calls. I don't know what else to do to get her to hear me out.

My eyes drift over the balcony and for a moment I wonder if it would hurt if I jumped. Will it take away the pain I feel at this moment? Contemplating if I should end it all, I hear voices in my living room. At this point I don't even care if someone is here to kill me.

Someone opens the patio doors. "We should have known you were here drowning your sorrows away," Ryan says.

"Jason, please come inside, it's cold out here," says Dianella.

I refused to move. It's not cold to me.

"Maybe we should let him be," says Knight.

Finally, someone with some sense.

"I am not leaving until he brings his ass in this house," Ryan says.

Well, I guess he needs to pack his bags, because I am not moving.

Ryan then throws a bucket of cold water in my face and I immediately jump up. "What the fuck, Ryan?"

"That got your ass up. Stop being a pussy and get in the house, or I will force you in the house."

Soaking wet, I walk into the house and head for my bedroom. Ryan follows me so I can't shut the door and lock it.

"Nice try, asshole. Get changed and bring your ass out here. We need to talk."

"Fine." Past pissed off, I reluctantly take my wet clothes off and put on some sweatpants and a t-shirt. I walk into the kitchen and pour me another drink.

Ryan snatches the drink out of my hand.

"Hey, I was drinking that."

"You've had enough to drink. Now sit down." I sit on the bar stool and place my head in my palms. I just want to be left alone. "Now that we have your attention, we are concerned about you."

"Yeah, I have never seen you like this before," Dianella says.

"Have you lost the love of your life because you're a fucking coward? You don't know how it feels to love someone, watch them go through the most horrific thing imaginable, and then put themselves in danger to save someone they don't even know. You don't, so don't judge me for how I feel or how I act. If I could change it all, I would do it in a heartbeat, but she refuses to take my calls."

"That is where you are wrong. Lily loves you too and she sacrificed herself to save others. That is the person she is. You cannot fault her for wanting to protect others. You do it every day too. You both do. Lily loves you and you love her. You need to man up and go to her if this is what you want, and I know that you do," Dianella says.

"It's easier said than done."

"If you sit here any longer, you will lose the best thing that has ever happened to you. I promise you that."

"How am I supposed to get her to listen to me?"

"Go to her. Talk to her. Make her listen."

"I really think you should go over there. You will find that Lily loves you more than you think. She's just scared. She feels that because of her she has lost everything she ever loved, starting with her parents and ending with you. The Page triplets were obsessed with her because of her parents dying. She hasn't really gotten over the fact that her parents were killed because she lost her memory. She had to relive that whole thing over again. Then she was stalked for years and girls were dying because she didn't catch on to the clues quick enough. She was then raped repeatedly, and you had to watch the brutal rape. She then offered herself to the same sick assholes to help more people and you had to watch that as well. She believes this is all her fault. She needed you and you pushed her away because you felt she was being defiant. You can't blame her for leaving. It's way too much for anyone to handle, let alone one person. She is a hero in my eyes. She is a badass detective who will always put others first. That is the person you fell in love with. You can't punish her for what she believes in or who she is," Knight says.

Knight is right. I need to correct this, and I need to do it now. I get up and head to the bedroom.

"Where are you going?" Dianella asks.

"I am going to get to get my butterfly back."

Chapter 34

Lily

I walk onto my back porch and sit in my favorite spot. I instinctively put my hands on my stomach. There are three other beings that I have to take care of now. What are the fucking odds that I am pregnant with triplets? I rub my stomach gently as if I can feel anything. I can't feel a thing, but I already feel a connection to my babies.

Oh my gosh, I am having babies, not baby. How the hell am I going to take care of three babies? It was hard enough raising my sister; now I am responsible for three other humans. This is crazy.

Deep down I can't help but think that I may be pregnant with three demons. I pray that I am not. I want these babies to be Jason's, not the people who raped me and beat me until I almost died. I need to find out before it is too late. The doctor said I could find out who the father is, but I need their DNA as well. That means I need to talk with Jason.

I hear the doorbell ring. It's probably one of my packages from Amazon. I've been reading a lot these days to pass the time. I get up and walk toward the front door.

Amelia answers it first. Once I see who it is, my heart drops into my stomach. I turn into a nervous wreck. He steps in with a strong, confident posture, just how I like, but I see a hint of fear in his eyes. He is afraid that I will tell him to leave.

I do the opposite and stand there speechless. Did Amelia tell him to come over? Did she tell him about the babies? I look at her with a horrified look in my eyes. She walks behind Jason and closes the door. She then mouths that she has no idea why he is here.

I let a deep breath out with a sigh of relief. Thank God she did not tell him. I have to be the one to tell him this news.

I speak first to encourage him. He looks like a terrified little boy who is about to get in trouble for breaking something. Will my kids look just like him? I hope so. "Hi Jason."

"Hi Lily, can we talk?"

Amelia excuses herself and walks upstairs.

"We can talk on the patio. Can I get you something to drink?"

"Yes, a glass of water please."

I pour him and myself a glass of water now that I can't drink anymore. I must keep my babies safe.

We walk through my bedroom to the patio and have a seat on the lounge chair. It feels so good outside, with the wind blowing and the chill coming in for fall season. I love the fall and springtime—the most beautiful times of year in Savannah. We sit in silence just absorbing each other's company.

"Jason—"

"Lily—"

"You go first." I say.

"I am so sorry, Lily. I never meant to hurt you. If anything, I should have been there for you when you needed me the most. If you give me another chance, I promise to always be there for you no matter what." He gets on his knees in front of me and places his head in my lap. He looks like a wounded boy who needs comforted. It must be the hormones because instinctively I start to stroke his hair. I want him to feel no pain.

He lifts his head and pleads with his beautiful green eyes. I see the sincerity in his gaze, and I know with all my heart he truly loves me and wants to be there for me. But when I tell him that I am pregnant with triplets, will he still have that sincerity, or will he leave me again? Only one way to find out.

"Jason, I don't forgive you, because you did nothing wrong. You made me promise to stay at work and stay away from the case, and I ignored your request. If anyone should apologize it should be me. I am sorry, Jason. I disrespected you and I promise I will never do that again. But do know that if I am passionate about something and I know that I am making the right decision, you must let me. I would never do anything to deliberately hurt you, but I will do what is right."

"I get that now. I know you are strong-willed, and you have a passion to protect others. That is why you are so good at your job. And I respect you for that. I love you for that." He reaches up with his palm and slides his fingers into my hair. He pulls me down into a kiss and at that moment I feel the electricity I've always craved. I feel the passion in his lips and the strength in his hold. I've missed this so much and I want it back more than anything, but I pull away. Our lips smack and he looks at me with a confused look on his face.

"I need to tell you something, Jason."

"Okay, you are scaring me. What is it?"

"I don't know how to say this, so I am just going to come out and say it. I'm pregnant. And it's triplets."

I witness the shock in his gaze, the confusion in his gaze, and the fear all at once. I know this is something he never wanted to hear. He mentioned so many times that other women tried to trap him for his money.

So, I continue because he is obviously speechless right now. "I know this is something you do not want to hear right now and please know I was as surprised as you are. I never thought this would be happening. But I am ten weeks pregnant. I found out a week ago and after the initial shock, I am actually happy about it. I know this is a lot for you to take in, and before you ask, I want a paternity test done now so I can find out if—"

He places a finger on my lips, stopping me from saying what we both are thinking.

"Lily, I love you and I am ecstatic that we will be parents. I don't need a paternity test because I know they are mine, but if you want one, I will do it in a heartbeat. Whatever you want, I am here for you."

I am shocked by his confession. He pulls me into a hug and embraces me for the first time in four weeks. His strong arms wrap around my waist and he pulls me in. I slide into his lap. His emerald eyes are burning with fire and I would know that look anywhere. He wants to make love to me, but he wants my permission first.

I look deep into his eyes and I whisper, "Make love to me, Jason. I want to feel all of you inside of me." That's all the confirmation he needs before he sweeps me off my feet and carries me into the bedroom. He places me gently on the bed because he thinks I am fragile now. He then takes my tights off. He lifts me up to remove my tank and bra. He takes off my panties. He then takes off his clothes and lays me back down on my bed and spreads my legs with his. He is moving incredibly slow, paying special care to me. He swipes his fingers over my clit and I nearly fall apart. I hear a deep grunt from within his chest and he inhales the smell of all of my essences.

"My god, you smell better than I could ever imagine before. I want you so bad, Lily."

"Then take me."

He then bends down and swipes his tongue over my clit and I immediately fall apart. I love it when he devours me with his tongue with such passion. He then lifts up abruptly and I feel lost without his pleasure. He pushes his large, thick dick inside of me and I scream out.

"Fuck, Lily. You are so tight. You feel so good, baby."

He starts to rock inside of me, and I feel the ecstasy increase with every stroke. His pelvic bone is rubbing on my clit and I don't know how much longer I can hold off.

"Give it to me, my love. That's right. Come for me."

I feel lightning shoot from my toes up into my fingers. I grab hold of Jason and dig my fingers into his back. He arches into me and I explode all around his dick. He continues to pump inside of me, and I know he is seconds from giving me his seed. He rocks harder and harder and then I feel his dick vibrate inside of me. He releases his seed, his essence, and for the first time in a long time, I feel truly satisfied. He gives me so much of his cum, it starts to run down my ass. He rolls off of me and cradles me in his arms. He looks into my eyes and I see pure, honest-to-god love in his gaze. This man loves me, and I love him.

"Lily, will you marry me?"

Epilogue
Nine Months Later

Jason

Lily is huge with my two boys and baby girl growing inside her. We decided to have the paternity test done and found that the babies are mine. It was the best news I ever received, second to her saying yes to marrying me. I am the luckiest guy in the world, and I wouldn't trade any of it.

Lily has been on bed rest for the past two months. The babies are growing healthy, but it is too much for her body frame. The doctor recommended that she stay at home for the duration of the pregnancy. Fine by me. I love seeing a pregnant woman walking around in my house. Well, our house now.

Lily wants to renovate her parents' house to be more practical for the kids. We agreed to raise our family in her parents' home. I just found out that it is finished and ready to move in, but I haven't told her yet. I want it to be a surprise. She wanted to wait to get married after we had the kids, but I want to bring my kids into this world the right way. So, I had Dianella and Amelia set up the backyard for a wedding and bought her a dress to wear over her large stomach. I love the way her hips spread and her breasts got bigger. I can't keep my hands off of her. We make love every day since we've been back together.

I walk into the bedroom and Lily is sprawled out on the bed. She looks so beautiful carrying my babies inside of her. "Lily, baby, it's time to get up. I need to run by the house to make sure everything is moving along. I want you to come with me."

She stretches her arms and legs. "Okay, give me a minute. These kids are kicking my ass." I laugh at her because it's so cute when she makes those facial expressions. She throws a pillow at me and I dodge out of the way. "It's not funny." I love her mood swings. They are a huge turn-on. "Wait till these little shits come out. It won't be so funny then."

"I love you, Butterfly, but you need to get up."

I walk out of the room and call Dianella and Amelia. "Is everything set up?"

"Yep, we are ready to go. We just need the bride and groom."

"We will be there in thirty minutes."

"Okay." They then hang up.

"I'm ready, but I feel like an elephant."

"You look beautiful, Butterfly."

"Whatever, I look like a cow."

"Whatever you say, baby, you look beautiful to me."

We head to the garage and get into the S500. I love Lily's car. We drive toward the house where the backyard has been transformed into a wedding sanctuary. On the way there, Lily starts to get uncomfortable.

"Are you okay?" I ask.

"Yes, they are kicking me again. I swear they hate me."

"They don't hate you. Our kids will love you. You will be a wonderful mother."

We pull up into the driveway. "Wow, how many people are working on this house? There are so many cars," Lily says.

"I have the very best because you deserve the very best."

We get out of the car and walk up to the front door. Lily takes her time because she is exhausted. I hope she makes it through the wedding. We open the door and Lily's eyes light up with excitement.

"Wow, this is amazing. They have really done a wonderful job. It looks exactly the way I want it. Thank you, babe."

"No need to thank me. I will always give you what you want."

Dianella and Amelia emerge from the kitchen looking fabulous.

"Wow, you two look amazing. Where are y'all going?"

"We are headed to a wedding but wanted to come see the renovations first."

Nice coverup, ladies.

"Come upstairs with us. We want to show you something." They grab Lily by the waist and the arm and help her up the stairs. That is my cue to go get dressed. Ryan should be in the master bedroom waiting for me. I step into the room and my tux is laid out for me. I immediately start to change.

"Hey, man, you ready for this?"

"I am more than ready. I've waited for this day my entire life. I've always wanted a family and now I will have one."

He pats me on the back. "You deserve to be happy. I am proud of you."

I finish getting dressed and step outside on the patio. Dianella and Amelia have really outdone themselves. There are all types of white flowers with white candles scattered everywhere. They created a sitting area for all the guests. It turned out to be a beautiful day with the sun setting just in time. I get in my place and shake the pastor's hand. He has been my pastor since I was a little boy. Big Mama would be so proud of me right now. I finally grew up into the man she wanted me to be. The soft music starts to play, and I look up.

I see the most beautiful woman walking toward me in the most beautiful white dress. Lily looks into my eyes and I see the tears running down her face. She had no idea that I planned all of this and now she is about to make me the happiest man on the planet.

She glides toward me like a butterfly drifting in the wind. The music is playing a soft melody and I am mesmerized by her beauty. She is pregnant with my kids and I couldn't be happier. We will finally be a family.

She places her hands in mine and I help her the rest of the way. The pastor then starts, and we exchange our vows. I place a ring on her finger. It's simple, yet elegant, just like her. Tears continue to flow down her cheeks and we finally say "I do."

"You may kiss your bride," says the pastor.

I reach for Lily's face and guide her lips toward mine. I then kiss her deeply, giving her all of me as she gives me all of her.

"I love you, Mrs. Lily Hall."

She lights up when she hears her name.

"I love you too, Mr. Hall." She then grunts and grabs her stomach. Her face turns with pain and she bends over. I hear a splash on the floor. "Shit, my water just broke," Lily announces. "Shit, I mean shoot."

Everyone scatters, trying to help. I scoop Lily into my arms and carry her to the car. She is panting because she is in pain and trying to breathe through it. The travel bag is already in the car because I wanted to be prepared. Ryan tosses the keys to me and Dianella and Amelia guide me to the car. I place Lily in the front seat, and I run to the driver side. I start the car and head to the hospital.

"It's okay, Lily, baby. You are doing good. Keep breathing like the classes taught you."

"Shhhiiitttt!" Lily yells. "This shit hurts bad. What the fuck was I thinking. I can't do this."

"Yes, you can, and you will. Those boys and our little princess need their mother. You can do this."

I make it to the hospital in record time.

"Okay, Ms. Matthews, it's time to push," says Dr. Lewis.

"It's Mrs. Hall now. Ahhhh," Lily corrects the doctor while pushing.

"Sorry, Mrs. Hall, now push," Dr. Lewis says.

"Uhhhhh. It hurts."

I let Lily squeeze my hand through all the contractions. "You are doing great, Lily."

"Fuck you, Jason. This shit hurts."

"Breathe, baby, breathe."

"I am breathing!"

"That's it. One more push and you can rest for a little bit."

She takes a deep breath and pushes as hard as she can.

"That's it. It's a boy."

"Jacob Hall. That's his name." My boy. Lily gave me my first boy.

Ten minutes later, Lily has to start pushing again. She is such a strong woman. I don't know of any woman as strong as her.

After three hard pushes, she delivers Johnathan Hall. My second boy.

"Okay, Lily. You have one more to go. You can do this."

"No, I can't. I am so tired." Her eyes start to close, sweat dripping from her forehead, and pure exhaustion written all over her face.

"I know you are, but you have to push one more time, okay?"

She then works up enough energy and pushes two more times. After the third push, Jasmine Hall greets us with beautiful hazel eyes. She looks just like Lily.

"Thank you, Butterfly. Thank you so much. This is the best gift you could have ever given to me in the world. I love you so much."

"I love you too." She then drifts off to sleep.

Three days later we are released from the hospital and head home. Jasmine, Jacob, and Johnathan sleep in a room together. They are so beautiful in my eyes. Jacob and Johnathan look just like me with green eyes and a strong jawline. Jasmine is the spitting image of her mother. She has wavy hair and beautiful skin. Lily did such a wonderful job.

Lily enters the nursery with me and starts to feed Jasmine first. She pulls her breast out and gives it to Jasmine. It's the most alluring thing I've ever seen. I have a newfound perspective of life now. I never wanted anything so much in my life. Lily has given me life, she has given me purpose, she has given me love.

She will have my heart until I leave this world.

"Lily."

She looks up with those beautiful eyes. "Yes?"

"You, Jasmine, Jacob, and Johnathan are my life. You mean the world to me and I promise to protect you all from everything this world throws at us."

"I know you will, and I will protect you too. I also wanted to let you know that I think I should take a break from police work. I don't think I will have the time to work and take care of the kids. I don't want anyone else raising my kids. It should be us."

That is the best news I've heard since the day she told me she was pregnant.

"That's fine with me. I will support you with whatever decision you make. I will always be here."

She lights up with happiness. She then places Jasmine back in the crib and picks up Johnathan. She breastfeeds him as well. She looks up at me with those beautiful hazel eyes.

"Jason, I love you."

"I love you too, Butterfly."